Also by Susanna Shore

House of Magic
Hexing the Ex
Saved by the Spell

P.I. Tracy Hayes
Tracy Hayes, Apprentice P.I.
Tracy Hayes, P.I. and Proud
Tracy Hayes, P.I. to the Rescue
Tracy Hayes, P.I. with the Eye
Tracy Hayes, from P.I. with Love
Tracy Hayes, Tenacious P.I.
Tracy Hayes, Valentine of a P.I.
Tracy Hayes, P.I. on the Scent

Two-Natured London
The Wolf's Call
Warrior's Heart
A Wolf of Her Own
Her Warrior for Eternity
A Warrior for a Wolf
Magic under the Witching Moon
Moonlight, Magic and Mistletoes
Crimson Warrior
Magic on the Highland Moor
Wolf Moon

Thrillers
Personal
The Assassin

Saved by the Spell

House of Magic 2

Susanna Shore

Crimson House Books

Saved by the Spell
Copyright © 2021 A. K. S. Keinänen
All rights reserved.

The moral right of the author has been asserted.

No part of this book may be reproduced, translated, or distributed without permission, except for brief quotations in critical articles and reviews.

This is a work of fiction. Names, characters, places, dialogues and incidents either are the product of the author's imagination or are used fictitiously. Any resemblance to actual events, organizations or persons, living or dead, except those in public domain, is entirely coincidental.

Book Design: A. K. S. Keinänen
Cover Design: A. K. S. Keinänen
Cover Image: Sergey Myakishev

ISBN 978-952-7061-47-3 (paperback edition)
ISBN 978-952-7061-46-6 (e-book edition)

www.susannashore.com

One

I RAN INTO A WOLF OUTSIDE MY BEDROOM. Not literally, or I wouldn't be here to tell the tale.

I was sleepwalking to the bathroom early Monday morning, and there it was, as if the hallway were a perfectly normal place for a woodland beast. My body froze in shock even as adrenaline surged through my veins, screaming for me to flee.

The conflicting commands were enough to jolt me wide awake.

The larger than normal grey wolf loped past me with an amused snarl—though I don't know how I could tell. Probably because I didn't get eaten.

My legs lost their ability to support me, and I leaned heavily against the doorjamb, heart beating like after a spin class that I'd recently started again and wasn't in shape for.

"Bloody hell, Ashley, you scared me to death."

The wolf sat calmly outside the bedroom next to mine and shot me a commanding look I had no trouble interpreting.

Gathering myself, I went to open the door for her. "You could've shifted, you know."

Ignoring me, the wolf entered her room and pushed the door closed with her head. I was alone in the hallway again, wondering if I'd imagined the whole thing.

A month ago, I would have had my head checked. That was before I'd moved into House of Magic and learned that I had a lot in common with Hamlet's Horatio. There definitely were more things in heaven and earth than I'd dreamt of in my philosophy. Such as it was.

House of Magic was a magic shop in Clerkenwell, Central London, the kind that sells herbal teas, tarot cards, and healing crystals for regular shoppers, and special ingredients for spells and potions for those in the know. Those would be mages.

The shop had been there for decades, but I'd only noticed it when I spotted a to-let sign in its window one memorable night. I'd been facing eviction, thanks to my then flatmate Nick, and in urgent need of a new place to stay. I'd thought it serendipitous that I'd been the first to notice the sign. But according to my landladies, there had been magic in play.

That's right, magic. Genuine, manipulating physics, no sleight-of-hand witchcraft and wizardry. The sign had been spelled to allow only the person who suited the house to see it. I'd been sceptical, to say the least.

Grateful, but sceptical.

Then I'd accidentally triggered a curse meant for my boss, Archibald Kane, and a whole new world had opened for me.

I'd learned that there truly was magic and people who were born to wield it. My landladies, Amber Boyle and Giselle Lynn, were mages. And to my utter shock, so was

Saved by the Spell

my boss whom I'd thought to be a perfectly boring antiques dealer. He was their leader even.

With the curse making my life difficult, I'd just about come to terms with magic existing. But then I'd learned that vampires and werewolves were real too, and that specimens of both were sharing the house with me.

One of them was Luca Marlow. He looked like a carefree Californian surfer about my age—twenty-six—with a muscled body and sandy hair in a short ponytail. But he was a vampire who had been alive for at least a century—if I believed his stories. His real age was shrouded in mystery.

Well, I'd refused to hear the truth.

And then there was Ashley Grant, the werewolf who had just given me the coronary. In human form she was a firefighter in her early thirties, easily tall and strong enough to pull off the job even without supernatural strength. With it, she was unstoppable.

I'd only seen her in wolf form once before, so it wasn't a wonder the encounter had shocked me. Maybe I should start keeping track of the full moon so that I'd be better prepared for the next time. But I hadn't expected her to run around the house as a wolf, full moon or not. Shouldn't they be a great secret?

I was still a little rattled when I entered the kitchen forty-five minutes later, after taking my time to calm myself and prepare for the day. I was wearing a new pair of blue jeans that hugged my legs and bottom in a becoming way—I noticed Amber check me out—and a light pink polka dot blouse with a large floppy bowtie at the front. I'd paired them with a brown corduroy blazer and knee-high leather boots. The day wasn't quite that chilly, but it was September in London; you never knew when it was going to rain.

Besides, it looked fabulous.

Giselle stood by the stove, making breakfast. The rent included meals—and chores—and she took care of cooking. Her excellent food was the reason I'd had to start spin classes again.

She was a tad over forty, short and round, with steel-grey pixie-cut hair, and a smiling countenance. She flashed me her dimples in greeting. "Morning, Phoebe. You look ready to face the new week."

I took a seat at the table. "Thanks. I don't feel like it. Ashley just gave me the shock of my life."

Amber grinned. A couple of years younger than her wife, she was pretty much the opposite of Giselle, tall and reed thin, with a shock of short red curls, and a stern demeanour that even a grin didn't properly soften.

"She takes a little getting used to in her other form. And it's good to be frightened. Just because she's not a threat to you doesn't mean other werewolves won't be."

A shiver went through my spine. "I'll try to avoid them."

"I've never met other werewolves than her, so chances are you'll never do either," Giselle consoled me as she placed a plate in front of me. "But I'm afraid having her in wolf form means there's no bacon today. I gave it all to her, because the wolf craves meat."

I dug in. "She's welcome to it."

"I usually reserve raw meat for her, but with the inventory at the shop, I completely forgot it's full moon."

"Can't she hunt for herself?" I asked, curious, not having come to think of this before. "London is full of rabbits. And there's deer in some parks."

Saved by the Spell

"They hunt when it's not the full moon, but during it they're too volatile to be allowed out of the house," Amber explained. "We lock her in the basement until morning so that she doesn't hurt anyone."

"But Luca lives in the basement." He had a sun-proofed studio there. He was sensitive to sunlight and slept during the day. But not in a coffin. I'd checked.

Giselle nodded. "He keeps an eye on her, makes sure she stays safe."

I tried to picture it. Luca was about an inch taller than my five-foot seven, tightly muscled and likely stronger than I believed, but Ashley had huge teeth and sharp claws in her wolf form. She'd make mincemeat of him in no time.

Then again, he'd protected me from a huge hellhound with magic, so maybe he could handle himself against her just fine.

I finished my baconless breakfast and, thanking Giselle, rose from the table to head to work. That roused Amber too.

"This waited for you in the post box. It must've been hand-delivered."

She gave me a heavy, cream-colored envelope that had my name and address written on it in professional cursive, but no stamp. My brows shot up.

"A wedding invitation?"

I ran through a list of friends in my head, but none of them had even hinted at that they'd be getting married. And I couldn't remember a casual acquaintance either who would be seriously involved with anyone. Curious, I opened the envelope and pulled out an elegant card with golden lettering.

Susanna Shore

The Right Honourable Hector Sanford and Lady Sanford are honoured to invite you to celebrate the engagement of their son Henry and Miss Olivia Radcliff at their home on Saturday, September 18th, at 6pm. RSVP by…

I stared at the invitation, blinking as I tried to make sense of it. I read the envelope again. It was most assuredly addressed to me, but I didn't know any Sanfords, no Henry, and definitely not any barons. Their address didn't ring a bell either, but it was in London, somewhere around Hampstead Heath, judging by the area code.

It wasn't until the third read that the name of the bride-to-be registered. My cousin Olivia.

Bloody hell.

My face must have shown my emotions because Giselle lifted her brows. "Not a happy invitation?"

I sighed. "It's an invitation to my cousin's engagement party. Actually, she's my cousin's daughter, but we're the same age, so it's always been more natural for me to think of her as my cousin instead of her mother."

Aunt Clara, Dad's older sister, had had her daughter in her early twenties, whereas my father had been over forty when I was born, so my actual cousin and I belonged to different generations.

"Olivia and I aren't close. I don't really understand why she's invited me. And judging by the fact that the event is this Saturday, she didn't do it voluntarily."

It wasn't pleasant to know that I'd been an afterthought, but that wasn't why the invitation dismayed me.

"My mother will not be happy that Olivia is getting married before me. She's a year younger."

Saved by the Spell

According to my parents, marriage was pretty much the only thing that I was good for. It aggravated me to no end, but since they lived in the south of France and I only saw them during holidays, I could ignore their opinions most of the time. But a wedding in the family would give Mom new wind for her demands.

I was currently single and not looking, so she could pester me all she liked. Nothing was going to change in a hurry.

I slipped the invitation into my tote to answer it during the day, and headed to work.

Monday morning, the Tube from Barbican Station at the north edge of the City was full of commuters, mostly businesspeople who worked in the City or Canary Wharf. I crammed myself into a train car and suffered the pressing bodies and jostling about. I switched lines at Liverpool Street Station and the pressure eased a bit, as most of the people continued east whereas I took the Central Line west.

Maybe it was the emptier car, maybe I was still jittery from the fright Ashley had given me, but halfway through my journey I started to feel like someone was watching me. It was like a pressure in my neck that wouldn't go away, an unpleasant sensation that made me want to hunch my shoulders to evade it.

As casually as possible, I turned to look behind me, but nothing caught my eye. The car was full of men and women in business casual, all keeping their eyes on the ads, their phones, or their feet as was proper. No one was staring at me.

I faced the door again and the sensation returned. It followed me out as I exited the train and climbed back on the street. Only there did the pressure ease, but I kept glancing back at every opportunity as I walked the last stretch of my commute.

Mayfair was on the west side of central London, the fashionable heart where aristocrats used to live and where all the luxury shops still were.

Kane's Arts and Antiques was located on a pedestrian court north of Oxford Street—technically in Marylebone—a little away from the tourist routes. You had to know it was there to find it, but we did excellent business.

The court was busy of people popping into the cafés along it to pick up their morning lattes on their way to work. Usually I wasn't one of them—there was a perfectly good coffeemaker at the office—but I needed something to calm my nerves. Coffee would do.

I chose a small place in the middle of the street, right opposite the gallery. It was my favourite café—their blueberry muffin was to die for—and it was relatively empty compared to the chain cafés on its sides.

I'd barely taken my place in the queue when a new customer entered and stepped behind me. The most delicious manly scent reached my nose, teasing my senses, conjuring images of handsome strangers.

I didn't want to turn to look, in case he was an octogenarian with good taste in colognes. That had happened to me before. I tried to spy him from the reflective surfaces in front of me, but all I could see was a tall form.

More people came in and he stepped closer to me. He wasn't quite touching me, but his nearness made my skin hum. My entire body became aware of him.

It was all I could think of. When it was my turn to order, I struggled to tell the woman behind the counter

Saved by the Spell

what I wanted. Luckily, she just asked if I wanted the usual, and I nodded, finding it easier than telling her I didn't want the muffin.

I fumbled in my tote for my purse, still painfully aware of the man. I pulled the purse out and promptly dropped it, spilling coins and cards everywhere.

My cheeks turned crimson as I hastily kneeled to gather everything. To make matters worse, he crouched to help me.

"Here, this should be everything."

The voice was wonderful, with a slight upper crust drawl, and the hand holding my cards was long-fingered and well-manicured. I lifted my gaze to his face—and forgot to breathe.

He had the most beautiful eyes I'd ever seen, so bright blue they seemed almost turquoise. The rest of him registered more slowly, the straight russet brows and the dimple that appeared on one side of his mouth when he flashed me a smile.

My fingers numb, I took the offerings. "Thanks," I managed to say as I rose back up. He rose too, steadying me from my elbow even though I didn't need it.

He was half a head taller than me, slim and dressed in business casual, blue jeans, white shirt, and black waistcoat under a black blazer. His dark russet hair was in careful disarray, and his features were delicate but defined enough to be manly.

I found him utterly handsome.

The dimple made another appearance. "My pleasure."

Fighting my embarrassment, I paid my purchases and moved to the other end of the counter to wait for my order. It arrived fast and I hurried out without a glance at the man.

I paused outside to gather myself, fanning my face to make the blush go away. I only had the pedestrian court to cross, but I didn't quite trust my legs to carry me.

"May I walk with you?"

I jumped as the rich voice spoke next to me. I hadn't even noticed that he'd followed me out. He was carrying a bag of muffins with no coffee, so he'd got his order fast.

"No, I … work over there." I nodded at the gallery and his brows shot up.

"You're a gallerist?"

"Assistant to one," I managed to say.

This was ridiculous. I could not lose my composure over a man like this. I inhaled deeply, straightened my spine, and gave him my most professional smile. "I have to go. Thank you for your help."

"At least tell me your name. I'm Jack."

"Phoebe."

He offered a hand, and I shook it. And like a cliché in every romance novel that I'd red—and I'd read a lot—a tingle spread form his hand to mine, spreading around my body.

"Lovely to meet you, Phoebe," he said with a warm smile, sketching a small bow over our joined hands. "I hope we'll meet again."

He released my hand and I muttered something incoherent before hurrying to the door that led to the offices above the gallery. I managed to fish out the key without spilling the contents of my bag, and open the door, but my hand shook when I entered the code to switch off the alarm.

The door closed behind me, and I leaned against it heavily. What a strange start to a week.

Good thing it couldn't get any stranger.

Two

I'D WORKED AT KANE'S ARTS AND ANTIQUES for two years, and I found my job interesting. I had a degree in art history and additional training at Sotheby's Auction House. My boss, Archibald Kane—or Kane as he'd asked me to call him, and can you blame him—allowed me to help him curate and organise exhibitions and auctions we held at the gallery. It was great education too.

Most of the time, however, I took care of the office as a glorified secretary.

This morning I couldn't care less if Kane got his morning tea on time. I dropped on my desk chair and took a long pull of my latte, trying to recover from the impact of Jack's eyes. My heart was coursing again, but not from fright. Exhilaration.

I was somewhat surprised by my reaction to him. I didn't usually lose my head over a handsome face, and I wasn't particularly needy for romance. I'd broken up with my previous boyfriend, Troy Nowell, three months ago and had only recently recovered from it.

Was this a reaction to Olivia's engagement? Was I that jealous of her happiness?

Disgusted with myself, I finished the coffee and went to make Kane his tea. I had it ready by the time he arrived, punctually at nine.

Archibald Kane was thirty-five going on a hundred and fifty, judging by his old-fashioned manners and inability to understand the modern world. He was tall and leanly muscled, with thick black hair that tended to billow as if powered by its own wind, deep blue eyes, and lean, defined face. He was handsome too, but I didn't lose my composure around him.

I was too intimidated by him to—though I was working on curing myself of that.

Like every day, regardless of the weather, he was dressed in a bespoke black three-piece suit and handmade leather shoes that were polished to perfection. His face was impeccably groomed, as if a beard were anathema to him.

He spotted me standing by my desk and I smiled in greeting. He paused to give me a look and his straight black brows furrowed slightly.

"Not a fan of jeans?" I quizzed. I'd worn jeans to work before, but I could never tell with him.

He tilted his head. "No … is there something new about you? Have you done something to your hair?"

I'd left my long cinnamon brown hair open today, but I'd worn it like this before too. "No. But the jeans are new."

"Hmmm…"

Without more comments, he went to his office and closed the door. I didn't take it personally. He often behaved abruptly.

Saved by the Spell

I had an auction to prepare, so I cast all men out of my mind, bosses and handsome strangers alike. It was three weeks to the auction, and I had tons of work to do. We always held good auctions, and I had reputation to maintain.

Kane left before lunch to check out an item that someone wanted to place in the auction. I took the opportunity to make a video call to my mom. Not that I was looking forward to it, but she'd be livid if I didn't inform her about the engagement.

My parents were having brunch on their back patio where the Mediterranean sun still shone warmly. They looked tanned and healthy. The move to permanent sun had been good for them after Dad had had a heart attack five years ago and had to give up running the family business. Aunt Clara's son-in-law, Olivia's dad, was the CEO now.

"Phoebe! It's not like you to call in the middle of the week. I hope nothing's amiss?" Mother was instantly worried. I grimaced.

"It depends on how you define it. Olivia's got engaged. They're holding a party this Saturday."

My mother pursed her carefully painted lips. She always looked impeccable, her strawberry blond hair and makeup perfect no matter the time of day. "Engaged? Olivia? And you only tell me now?"

"I only received the invitation today."

Mom glared at Dad. "Did you know about this?"

"I had absolutely no idea," he assured her calmly. He was seventy-three and his cinnamon hair had turned mostly white. I took after him, except for my brown eyes that came from Mom. "Who is the fellow? Anyone we know?"

"Henry Sanford. Son of Baron Sanford."

Mother's brows shot up. "Baron? How is it possible for Olivia to get engaged to a baron's son and Clara not to gloat about it immediately?"

I hadn't come to think of that. "Maybe she's pregnant?"

Mom's eyes grew large, and Dad cleared his throat, as if to hide his embarrassment—or snickering. "It's not considered scandalous anymore you know," Mom said. "That's not a reason for a hasty marriage."

Having children outside marriage hadn't been a scandal in decades, but I didn't point it out. "Maybe the entire family only learned now?"

"I'll have to call Clara," Mom declared. "And you'll have to represent the family. Dress appropriately."

I promised to do so and ended the call. It had gone better than I'd hoped. She hadn't asked once why I wasn't getting married.

I rejoiced too early. Mother called back half an hour later. "You were right. Clara was flabbergasted by the engagement. Olivia hadn't spoken about it to anyone, and they all received the invitation today. The family is not happy."

"Even though she's marrying a baron's son?" I asked blithely.

"Clara doesn't know the family."

And that was the greatest condemnation there was.

Mom gave me a pointed look. "Are you seeing anyone?"

Annnnd there it was. I'd almost escaped.

"I've barely recovered from Troy." I tried to sound calm and reasonable, but I was irritated.

"You're not getting any younger."

Saved by the Spell

I would've rolled my eyes if we weren't on video call. "I know. And I can promise that I'll tell you the moment I contemplate marriage to someone. No secret engagements for me."

"You'd better," she sniffed. "This is not at all how things are done."

I kept wondering about the engagement long after the call ended. Why would Olivia keep it a secret? Unlike me, she'd always aimed for a marriage, as if she didn't have a good job at a law firm on top of her daddy's money. I wouldn't rule out pregnancy, no matter what Aunt Clara said.

Kane returned in the afternoon with an ugly orange and white acrylic table lamp. His deep blue eyes were shining as he showed it to me.

"I've been looking for this. Finnish design from 1950s. Difficult to find around here. I'll put it in the auction, but I've a half mind to bid for it myself."

I stared at the hideous thing with my mouth open. I'd visited his home once and it was mostly decorated in Danish mid-century modern of elegant cherrywood and white upholstery. The lamp would fit the place like a werewolf in my hallway.

"Is it expensive?"

"They go around a thousand pounds, a bit more in auctions."

Pleased with himself, he carried the lamp to his office. With a sigh, I followed him so that I could photograph the lamp for the catalogue. I'd seen odder items during my time here—and that wasn't even including the curse statuette.

~ ~ ~

I'M NOT A TRAINED PHOTOGRAPHER, but I'd learned to take catalogue worthy photos of the items we were auctioning.

We had a small "studio" set at the side of Kane's office with a proper lighting and neutral background. I'd even learned to operate the complicated camera that was permanently set on a tripod.

Kane most assuredly wouldn't bother to learn it, so I'd had to. I don't know who photographed for him before I joined the firm, but it wasn't him.

That didn't stop him from paying close attention to what I was doing, his mouth pursed with displeasure. I was growing anxious, and I kept glancing at my camera settings and the lights in case they were incorrect.

Or maybe he feared I wouldn't show the ugly lamp to its advantage.

He cleared his throat. "I've been racking my brain over what's wrong with you."

That was not what I thought he'd say.

I straightened and shot him a dismayed look. "Excuse me?"

He studied me with a puzzled frown, impervious to my reaction. "I think it's something magical. Every time I look at you, a wave of repulsion washes over me, and that's not a normal reaction for me."

"What?"

I was unable to fathom his words. Magic, again?

He tilted his head, his jaw tightening as he tried to look at me. "You're an attractive woman. I should want to look at you. Yet even now, I have to force myself."

He stepped backwards, shuddering.

"Has anything unusual happened to you lately?"

Saved by the Spell

I struggled to gather my thoughts, stunned by his behaviour. "You mean since the curse meant for you was lifted?"

He shook his head. "More recent than that. Over the weekend, maybe? I would've noticed if it had taken place earlier."

I gave it a thought. "I went to shopping with friends on Saturday. Nothing extraordinary happened."

I'd had a great time with my girlfriends, and I'd bought these jeans, among other things.

"Any new friends among them?"

"No. I've known all three since university."

He tapped his mouth with a finger. "Hmm..."

"This morning, however, was full of odd things," I told him, counting with my fingers. "I saw a werewolf, I was invited to my cousin's out-of-the-blue engagement party, and then at the Tube I felt someone staring at me. Not like in passing. It was really intensive, physical sensation."

That got his attention. "Did anyone touch you there?"

I rolled my eyes. "It's the Tube in morning rush. Everyone touched me."

"Maybe it was something that happened there..."

"Never mind where," I huffed. "I'm more interested in why? Have I been cursed again?"

"I don't know." He ran fingers through his billowing hair, aggravated. "I don't think I'm able to figure it out alone. We need Giselle and Amber. Let's go."

He had barely patience to wait for me to fetch my belongings before leading me to his car, a red Jaguar he kept in a reserved spot in a multistorey car park near the shop—that is to say, only three streets away.

I'd seldom had a chance to ride in it, but it wasn't as exciting as one might think. The insides were rather small, and London traffic didn't allow the car to shine.

The tight space proved more aggravating than usual, as Kane had to sit next to me the whole ride. His face was growing paler by the mile, and sweat was glistening on his forehead. Whatever it was that was affecting him—could it really be me?—had to be bad.

We reached the House of Magic before he had to throw up, and he escaped the car like it was on fire. He hurried to the back entrance, for once eschewing his usual polite manners, and I followed him into the shop. Amber was there and she smiled when she spotted us.

"Archibald. You haven't been here since the curse was lifted."

He smiled in return and inclined his head in a small bow. "I've been somewhat busy with the leadership contest."

He hadn't mentioned it to me. In fact, he had behaved like the curse never happened and I'd never learned about magic. Today was the first time he'd brought it up again. Trust it to be because I'd been bespelled again.

She propped her hip against the counter. "Anyone giving you trouble?"

"No one yet, but I've needed to settle smaller disputes."

"So what brings you here today?"

Kane turned to indicated me. "I think someone's put a spell on Phoebe and I have no idea what it is."

This caught her interest. She leaned toward me, as if taking a sniff. "I can't sense anything."

Saved by the Spell

Kane startled. "That's odd. It's all I can sense when I'm around her. It's as if there's a field around her designed to make her repulsive."

Amber glanced at her wristwatch. "Let me check if Luca is awake yet and able to man the shop."

"It's daylight still," I reminded her. We'd left the gallery early, and even though the drive had been slow, it was barely past four.

"I think he might manage, with the sky overcast like this," she said, disappearing into the backroom, where steps led down to the basement and Luca's sun-proofed studio.

Turned out, she was right. Only moments later, Luca climbed up, looking a bit bleary, as if he'd just woken up, but already dressed up and his hair in a tiny bun. He grinned when he spotted me, then pulled back with a frown.

"Is there something … wrong about you?"

"Not you too," I huffed, but Kane was instantly alert. "You can sense it as well?"

Luca stepped closer to me and his nose twitched in distaste, as if I reeked. "It's like you've turned repulsive all of a sudden."

I threw my hands up. "That's just great. I'm spelled to disgust people?"

"Let's not make hasty conclusions," Amber said. "I'm not disgusted by you."

"We'll find out what it is," Kane stated, gesturing for us to proceed upstairs before him.

Giselle was in the kitchen with Griselda, the grey cat who reigned supreme over us, pouring cat food into a bowl even though it should be hours until feeding time. The cat was winding around her legs impatiently. Giselle straightened when she spotted us, smiling delighted when she spotted my boss.

"Archibald! What a pleasant surprise. You'll stay for dinner?"

"Absolutely," he said, pleased. "But we have a small problem that needs to be dealt with first."

"Oh?"

"Apparently there's a curse on me again," I growled, and her brows shot up.

"How did that happen? What sort of a curse?"

"Luca and I are suddenly finding her very off-putting," Kane told her, "but Amber isn't affected."

Like the others earlier, Giselle came to me and studied me carefully. She touched my face and even took a sniff. I suffered it gracefully.

"I can't detect anything."

"Maybe it's gender specific…" Kane mused. "Do you have anything that we could use to detect what kind of spell it is?"

"Let's go upstairs and see."

I followed them up, my annoyance evident in every stomping step. I'd been wrong this morning. It was, in fact, possible for my week to turn stranger.

Three

AMBER AND GISELLE HAD SET THE ATTIC as a workspace for their mage stuff and preparing the ingredients they sold in the shop. It was an open space with a polished wooden floor and skylights that gave to both sides of the building on the slanted ceiling. Shelves lined the walls, filled with herbs, potions, candles, and other ingredients they needed in their spells. A wooden worktop was placed under one skylight facing the street.

I followed Giselle to the worktop, where mortars of different sizes were placed in a neat row, with cauldrons and a gas burner, knives and scissors, spoons and ladles in old jars. Amber and Kane went to a shelf that held old books and began to pull them out one by one to skim the contents.

"I need a lock of your hair," Giselle said to me. She took scissors and cut a few long strands near my skull. "That shouldn't be noticeable."

I hoped so.

She dropped the hair into a small mortar. Then she pulled out jars and vials from the shelves, seemingly at random, and put a pinch or drop from each into the mortar too. When the ingredients were in, she took a pestle and ground everything into pulp. Once the consistency was to her liking, she took a bottle full of emerald-green liquid and poured some over the pulp until it was completely covered.

To my amazement, it turned clear almost immediately. Not even the pulp was visible anymore. Giselle made a decisive nod.

"Definitely a spell, not a curse."

My shoulders slumped, as if I'd held a hope that nothing was amiss. At least it wasn't a curse this time round, not that I could immediately fathom how that made a difference for me. "What kind of spell?"

Giselle shook her head. "I have no idea."

That was encouraging.

Griselda jumped on the worktop and pushed her head into the mortar to drink the liquid. I hastened to remove her, but Gis smiled.

"No worries. It's water."

I placed the cat on the floor where she proceeded to lick her paws. "Water? You put all sorts of stuff in there and now it's water?"

"That's how I know you've been spelled. If it had been a curse, smoke would've risen from it."

Kane came to us, carefully keeping Giselle between us. It should not have upset me, but it did. He was holding a leather-bound book from maybe the seventeenth century, judging by the quality of the paper and the print work. He had it open on a page he showed us.

"I think it's a protection spell. This one describes exactly how I feel."

Saved by the Spell

"Protection against what?" I asked amazed and he grinned.

"Men."

Giselle and I stared at him with mouths open. "What?"

His eyes crinkled at the corners as he smiled. "This describes a medieval spell that fathers put on their maiden daughters to protect them against unwanted attention from men, and husbands on their wives to keep them faithful."

Giselle nodded, her mouth in a grim line. "Trust men to want a spell like that. So how do we break it?"

Kane looked apologetic. "It doesn't say. It doesn't even say how it was cast in the first place. It only gives me the name of the spell."

I groaned. "What use is that book, then?"

He glanced at me from under his brows, the closest he could come to look at me. It was as if its effect on him was growing worse.

"It tells me the spell exists and where I can start looking for it. The council headquarters should have the grimoire I need."

"Is there any chance you'd go look for it immediately?" I suggested hopefully. "I have an engagement party to attend to this weekend and I don't want to repel half the guests there."

"Oh?" He hesitated. "Not yours I presume?"

I rolled my eyes. As if I wouldn't tell him if I became engaged. "My cousin's."

"Ah." He glanced at his watch. "I guess I could go tonight."

"Not before you've had dinner," Giselle stated firmly, pushing me gently towards the door.

27

Ashley was in the living room when we returned there, lying on the sofa, her long legs hanging over the armrest. She wore soft black jogging bottoms and a matching hoodie with the logo of London Fire Brigade on the front. Her bald head was glistening with sweat, and she'd thrown an arm over her eyes.

"Should you be up yet?" Amber asked worried, going to check on her. She was a former A&E nurse, so taking care of people came naturally to her, even if her stark demeanour suggested otherwise.

"The evening after full moon always feels like the world's worst hangover," Ashley said, her voice feeble. "But I need food, so I might as well get up."

In due course, we sat at the table. Ashley joined us, even though she was still pale, which meant that Griselda was a no-show. The cat knew exactly what Ashley was and didn't like it.

Luca arrived too, having closed the shop for the duration. It would be opened again for the night customers at eight. I'd wondered at the odd hours when I moved in here, but maybe vampires came to the shop often and needed convenient hours.

My mind was briefly occupied with the problem of how vampires shopped for groceries. Maybe they had everything delivered.

It was an odd dinner, with Luca and Kane avoiding looking at me. I sat at the other end of the long table from them and didn't make them so sick they couldn't have done justice to Giselle's stew.

Ashley ate twice as much as the rest of us combined, so I guess her nausea had passed too.

Saved by the Spell

"Are you two angry with Phoebe?" she asked the men when she'd recovered enough to pay attention to her surroundings.

I pursed my lips, aggravated. "Apparently I have a protection spell on me that makes me repulsive to men."

She threw her head back and barked a loud laugh. "How the fuck did that come about? Do you have an overprotective father? A jealous boyfriend?"

"Neither, nor do I know any men who can do magic except these two, and I'm fairly sure they're not responsible."

Kane and Luca shook their heads enthusiastically.

"So where did it come from?" Luca asked.

I'd avoided thinking about it thus far. I spread my arms. "I have no idea. Could it be a residue of the curse?"

The curse I'd triggered had made everything I wished on others to come true. Even nice wishes had twisted so that they made the other person's life difficult, on top of which every wish had bounced back to me and I'd effectively cursed myself too.

"I wished that Ashley would be safe at work. Maybe it's bouncing back again?"

All the mages at the table shook their heads. "It's not a curse," Giselle said. "It's positive, benign magic."

"That makes me repulsive?"

"Only to men," Amber consoled me, and then added with a teasing smile: "You could switch teams."

"If I were at all attracted to women, I would," I said sourly, making the women laugh. Giselle patted my shoulder.

"Well then, until we figure out how to remove the spell, enjoy the added safety it gives you."

~ ~ ~

EXACTLY HOW SAFE I WAS from men became evident the next morning. The Tube car was as full of people as always, but today I had more breathing room than before. Consciously or not, the men around me kept a careful distance, no matter the discomfort for themselves. Not a single body bumped against me, accidentally or intentionally.

I could get used to this.

Central Line was emptier again, though not so much so that I would have been able to sit, but I had a good spot near the door at the front of the car.

The train had barely left the station when the pressure in my neck returned, same as the previous day. Determined to locate the source, I swirled around, glaring at the general direction where the sensation came from. But no one was looking at me, and I only managed to startle the woman behind me.

I leaned over to peer behind her, but I spotted no one. Could someone be watching me on the CCTV? But there were those on every line, yet I only felt it here.

When I turned to face the front again, the sensation returned, and it remained even though I tried to keep people between me and the direction it came from.

It wasn't until I exited the Tube station that the sensation eased, but I couldn't relax. Could it be a side effect of the curse? Sorry—*spell*. I wouldn't be surprised if it contained a possibility that the commissioner—aka the overprotective father/jealous husband—would want to keep an eye on his daughter or wife.

That wasn't creepy at all.

By the time I reached the pedestrian court outside the gallery, I desperately needed a consoling latte. I wouldn't mind a glimpse of the turquoise eyes either…

Saved by the Spell

I was already heading to the café when I realised that he would be repelled by me too. My shoulders slumped in disappointment, and I swerved to the office instead, my steps slow and heavy. I was feeling sorry for myself as I prepared for the day.

My mood didn't improve when Kane arrived. One glance told me he hadn't located the spell.

"Don't despair yet," he consoled me, as he hurried past me to his office. "We have a huge library. Every benign spell is there. I just have to locate it."

"Someone has to know about the spell already," I pointed out. "How else could they have cast it?"

He nodded approvingly. "Excellent point. I'll ask around. Meanwhile, you should try to figure out who would want to do this to you and why."

"It's not for my protection, that's certain."

He paused at his door. "It does seem to have a malicious intention, as it's making your life more difficult. Are you perhaps courting the same man as some other woman? Maybe she's spelled you so he wouldn't notice you?"

The thought had merit, even though I'd never "courted" anyone in my life. "I'm not currently seeing anyone."

Memory of the turquoise eyes made my insides warm. Maybe he had a jealous stalker who spelled any woman who so much as glanced at him. I couldn't remember that there would've been anyone around us, but then again, I'd been completely unable to pay attention to anything but him.

"Could it be Danielle again?" I suggested instead.

His ex-wife, Danielle Mercer, had been under the impression that Kane and I were romantically involved, one of the reasons she'd laid the previous curse on me.

He grimaced, looking uncomfortable. They hadn't really resolved their issues after the divorce, and while he couldn't accept the direction her pursuit of power had taken her, on some level he still cared for her.

"She'd make sense, and she definitely has the skills." She was studying dark magic with a warlock, an evil mage who practiced death magic and had shed his humanity for power and longevity. "But she hasn't been sighted in London since she left with that French chap."

The "chap" was Laurent Dufort, the warlock who was teaching her. He was mind-numbingly attractive for an evil non-human who was presumably over a hundred and fifty, and the two were an item—or at least had been before she left him and stole his curse statuette. It could be Danielle was happy with him and had better things to do than to mess the imaginary relationship between Kane and me.

"What about the engagement party you mentioned?" Kane asked.

"That's for my cousin Olivia. We're not close and I don't even know the fellow."

"What's his name? Maybe he's from a mage family."

"Henry Sanford."

He shook his head. "Not anyone I know. I don't think there's a mage family named Sanford, in London anyway, but I can check if there's one elsewhere."

I sighed. "It would be weird if Olivia had put a spell on me so her fiancé wouldn't notice me. She doesn't know about magic, and it would've been much easier for her simply not to invite me to the party."

Saved by the Spell

He agreed to that and then disappeared into his room. His face was tight, the strain of talking with me this long evident.

An hour later, I received a message from Mom informing me that she'd arranged a fitting for me that afternoon for an engagement party dress at the Dior boutique. I wasn't exactly a Dior kind of girl, but I had nothing against a good cocktail dress, especially since she was paying.

I tried to make do with my salary, instead of relying on my parents' wealth, but I never said no to Mom if she wanted to buy me clothes. Usually, generous purchases like that came with lectures on my marital status. But since I would receive one anyway—thanks to Olivia—I might as well enjoy the perks.

The Dior boutique was on New Bond Street, a half a mile from the gallery. I told Kane I'd be gone for longer than usual on my lunch break, much to his relief, and set out on foot.

Mom had given instructions for the dress when she made the appointment, and her notion of a perfect dress sadly differed from mine. A dozen dresses were waiting for me when I arrived, all suitable for a society matron twice my age.

I stared at them in horror. "I am not trying those on."

The shop assistant nodded. "Maybe we could compromise," she said tactfully.

And that's what we did. I emerged from the boutique with a dark blue silk cocktail dress that had a flouncing pleated hem which reached my mid-calf and continued diagonally up the fitted strapless top. A narrow black belt brought it together. It was a perfect blend of elegant and youthful.

Pleased with my purchase, I returned to the gallery to show the dress to Mrs Walsh, who was in charge of the customer side of the shop. She was in her mid-fifties, and half a head shorter than me even in four-inch heels. She was a great connoisseur of haute couture who always wore designer clothes and genuine jewellery, and she gave me her approval for the dress.

I was about to head back upstairs when a customer walked in. He was past sixty, tall, with snow-white hair, and dressed in tweed. He nodded at Mrs Walsh and then turned to me. His white bushy brows furrowed, and he shook his head before addressing Mrs Walsh.

"I'd like to see the lot number thirty-four."

The auction items were on display in the adjacent exhibition space for people to peruse before the event. Since the auction was my purview, I smiled and stepped closer.

"This way, sir."

I gestured with my hand for him to precede me, and he did, making sure to give me a wide berth. I led him to the correct item and then took pity on him and retreated. He didn't linger at the display and left without any word about whether he would attend the auction.

Bugger.

"What was that about?" Mrs Walsh asked, baffled, when the door closed behind him.

I gave a nonchalant shrug. "Maybe he thought I'm too young to know anything. Next time you handle him."

The moment I was back upstairs, I marched to Kane's office. "The spell is repelling customers too. You have to do something before I lose my job."

Saved by the Spell

He gave me a distracted smile, his attention on his computer. "I'd be a poor boss if I fired you for something you have no power over."

But since he couldn't look directly at me, I knew it was only a matter of time before he changed his mind.

He was hopeful he'd find a solution that evening. "I'll let you know the moment I have it," he told me when we closed at the end of day.

But despite his optimism, he had only disappointing news for me the next morning, and every morning after that. And before I knew it, it was Saturday.

Four

AUNT CLARA WAS WAITING FOR ME in the magic shop when I descended the stairs at the appointed time. She was studying the place curiously while regaling Amber with a story of the latest disaster her bones had predicted, a flash flood in Indonesia.

Amber listened politely. Customers like Aunt Clara were inevitable when one ran a magic shop.

Aunt Clara was four years older than my father and looked a lot like him too, tall, thin, and commanding. I guess I did as well—except for the commanding part. Her hair wasn't white like his, but I suspected the cinnamon colour we shared was a courtesy of her hairdresser—unlike mine.

She always dressed in Chanel and tonight wasn't an exception. Her black cocktail dress was timeless and age-appropriate, if it applied to a woman nearing eighty. Her pearl necklace was a gift from her late husband, and she always wore it too.

She gave me a sharp look when I entered the shop. "You could've worn more jewellery."

I took that as an approval of my looks since she couldn't find anything else to complain about.

I was happy with them myself. My makeup and hair were done by professionals—a rare indulgence—and the cameo choker I'd inherited from my grandmother, Aunt Clara's mother—which I guess was the cause for her complaint—suited the dress perfectly.

I pressed my cheek against hers in greeting. "How come you're not going with Emilia and John?" They were Olivia's parents.

"I promised your mother I'd make sure you won't embarrass the family."

I rolled my eyes. As if I'd never been to a society event before. But I was glad for her company, so I kept my mouth shut. Her presence might make the curse—fine, *protection spell*—less noticeable too. People would naturally interact with her and ignore me.

It was a six-mile drive north to Hampstead Heath. The Sanford family lived on the north-western edge of the heath, right by the park. A footpath led into a copse of woods at the end of their street and there were trees everywhere, golden and red in the setting sun.

The house was a late eighteenth-century cottage, a rambling brown-brick with white trimmings around its small-paned windows. A garage wing had been added at some point, but it too was so old you couldn't really tell the difference between the original house and the addition.

Aunt Clara nodded approvingly. "At least they have money. You never know with these aristocrats."

I bit my lip to keep myself from commenting and hoped she wouldn't bring it up with Olivia's future in-laws.

Saved by the Spell

Another black cab pulled over behind us and Olivia exited with her parents. She was a dainty woman with honey blond hair and large periwinkle blue eyes that made her look perpetually innocent. Men always thought she was a delicate creature in need of protection, and she was good at playing to their notions.

She looked radiant in a light pink silk dress that was pleated diagonally similarly to mine, except that her top had cap sleeves. She hugged her grandmother carefully and then kissed the air on both sides of my cheeks.

"Congratulations," I said warmly. "Quite a surprise you gave us."

She showed her hand that had a huge diamond ring on it, and I made appropriate noises. "Harry managed to surprise me too. We've only been dating for two months."

Okay…

I greeted Emilia—my actual cousin and a younger copy of Aunt Clara—and her husband John, a tall man in his mid-fifties who ran the family business. Emilia complimented my looks and John frowned and pulled back. He was usually a nice man, but I knew it was the spell causing it and didn't take it personally.

The double gates in the brick wall that separated the front garden from the street were open, with braziers burning invitingly on both sides. With Olivia going in first and me keeping the rear, we made it down the paved path to the main door, where we were greeted by Baron and Lady Sanford.

He was closer to sixty than fifty and had the air of a college professor about him, his thin hair slightly dishevelled and his manners absentminded. She was about a decade younger, American, and judging by the jewellery she'd caked herself with, the money.

They were happy and cordial, and surprised but pleased by the sudden engagement. We were then introduced to the groom to be. He was about my age, a tall and elegantly dressed man who resembled his father with his light brown hair and friendly eyes.

I braced myself when it was my turn to greet him, but he was too well-brought-up to show his reaction, though the handshake was brief. If Olivia noticed, she didn't comment.

I was almost certain she hadn't put the spell on me.

We were led deeper into the house as more guests began to arrive. It was as rambling on the inside as it was on the outside, and crammed full of antique furniture and art. I was instantly fascinated, and could have spent the evening studying the place, the gallerist in me putting a price tag on everything.

I guess I was as bad as Aunt Clara.

Unfortunately, she knew me well, and she pulled me into a large parlour where other guests were gathering. In my aunt's wake, I made the rounds, gracefully suffering the shudders and distaste of every man. If Aunt Clara noticed their snubs, she didn't comment.

The evening progressed smoothly. There were drinks and finger food, and I concentrated on the latter so that I wouldn't have to speak with anyone. I wasn't a natural recluse, but I didn't want to ruin the evening for anyone.

When it was time for the speeches and toasts, I retreated to the back of the parlour, where I could observe without offending. All the right words were said, no one brought up the hasty engagement, and the young couple looked radiantly happy. I tried not to envy them.

"Do you think she's pregnant?" a woman about my age asked in a quiet tone by my ear. She was taller than

Saved by the Spell

me, with short-cropped shock-red hair from the bottle, and laughing grey eyes. I vaguely recalled that she was Henry's cousin from his father's side.

I grinned. "It's always possible, but would they even know yet? They've been together for such a short time."

She tilted her head sideways in acknowledgement. "I'm Ida Sanford, by the way, Harry's cousin." So I'd remembered correctly.

"Phoebe Thorpe. I'm Olivia's mother's cousin."

"Huh. There's an age difference. Are your parents here?" She glanced around.

"No, they live in Southern France."

Her face turned wistful. "I wish I were living there. So … when's the wedding, you think?"

"If it's soon, we'll know she's pregnant," I said dryly.

She laughed aloud, making the people glare at us, because the groom's father was speaking. We ducked our heads and snickered to ourselves.

The moment the speech was over, Ida took me by the arm. "Come meet the younger generation."

I followed her to the adjoining room where the friends of Olivia and Henry had gathered, and Ida introduced me to everyone. The spell hadn't mysteriously been lifted and all the men turned away from me the moment they could. It miffed me more than with the older family members, because there were a couple of men among them that I might have been interested in.

"What's going on with you and the men?" Ida asked, amazed. She was more astute than I'd hoped.

"I have a spell on me that makes me repel men," I said with a deadpan tone, opting for truth since I had no other explanation for it. She laughed aloud.

"More for me."

There definitely wouldn't be anyone for me. Even if the spell were suddenly lifted, the men would remember their initial dislike of me.

Feeling sorry for myself, I was ready to retire when a familiar voice spoke behind me.

"Phoebe? What are you doing here?"

~ ~ ~

I SWIRLED TO FACE THE beautiful turquoise eyes I'd reminisced about more than I should have this past week. "Jack?"

I couldn't believe he was here.

"You remember my name."

Warm smile made his eyes twinkle as he studied me with appreciation. I held my breath, but the smile didn't turn to disgust. I didn't dare let down my guard though. It would be doubly disappointing if he was repulsed by me.

"I didn't notice you earlier."

Smooth, Phoebe.

He made a vague gesture with his hand. "I arrived when the speeches had already begun and remained by the door. Are you family?"

"Olivia's," I explained, and he nodded.

"Harry and I have been best friends since Oxford. I guess we'll be seeing more of each other from now on?"

"I guess so," I said with a breathless smile. I'd become best friends with Olivia if it kept me near him.

He lifted his empty glass and pointed at mine that was almost empty too. "Would you like another glass of wine?"

Saved by the Spell

I nodded and he left to fetch more. I waited with my shoulders tense, fearing that he'd have a belated reaction to the spell when he returned.

"Ah, Jack Palmer..." Ida said, materialising next to me. "He's a lovable scamp, so watch out."

He could be the worst womaniser in the world as long as he saw me and didn't become nauseated. And that was even though my previous boyfriend had broken my heart by cheating on me.

Jack returned with two glasses. He gave one to me and then handed the other to Ida with a polite bow. "I'll fetch one more."

I was thoroughly charmed by his courtesy, making Ida roll her eyes.

"That's how they get you..."

I shooed her away when I saw Jack return, and she left with a grin. If he wasn't affected by the spell, I didn't want her around to ruin my chances, and if it had taken effect while he was away, I didn't want her to witness my disappointment.

But his smile was as open as before, his gaze frank on me. "Alone at last..."

I grinned. "Hardly."

There were so many people attending the party that we were constantly jostled about as people moved from room to room.

His answering grin brought out the dimple on his cheek. "We could leave."

"Tempting..." And it truly was. If I hadn't been here for my family, I would've left instantly.

He propped a shoulder against a wall, blocking us in. "So how have you been this week?"

I had a mad urge to tell him about the spell. "Busy. We're organising an auction."

"Anything interesting on sale?"

"That depends, do you like mid-century modern?"

"I don't even know what that means," he confessed with a self-deprecating laugh.

In a normal situation, I would've counted it against him, but he was so charming I barely noticed. Standing close, I could detect his delicious scent. My mouth went dry, and I took a hasty sip from my glass.

Harry and Olivia came to us. He held back, his brows furrowing in a puzzle as he tried to figure out why he didn't like me, but she wrapped an arm around me, as if we were close friends, looking giddy.

"I love this dress," she stated. "You'll have to wear it to the wedding. It's exactly the colour I want for my bridesmaids."

My mouth almost dropped open. "You want me to be one of them?"

"Of course. You're the closest thing I have to a sister."

Okay…

I wasn't exactly looking forward to it, but I smiled and said I'd be honoured. "When's the wedding?"

"Two weeks from now. I know it's fast, but we couldn't wait." She must have noticed my expression, because she gave me a fed-up look. "I'm not pregnant."

"Good to know…" Then I frowned, as her words registered. "Wait, what's the exact date?" She told me and I cursed aloud. "We have an auction that day."

She pulled her short body straight. "Surely my wedding is more important?"

"Of course it is…"

Kane might take some convincing though.

Saved by the Spell

Pleased, she left with Henry to greet other guests. Jack smiled at me. "We're going to have so much fun at the wedding. I'm the best man."

My heart skipped a beat. "That's nice."

"And I absolutely agree with your cousin: you look lovely in that dress." His gaze was intimate, and I felt a blush rise.

"Thank you," I managed to say.

We talked about this and that, and he didn't even hint that he should talk with other people too. It seemed like a moment later that Aunt Clara came to look for me.

"The cab is almost here. I'll see you home."

Jack looked disappointed. "I could've escorted you."

"Thank you, but I'll have to go with my aunt," I said with true regret.

"So when can I see you again?"

My breath caught. "I … am free most evenings."

"How about tomorrow afternoon? I'll take you to lunch. Let's meet at Brasserie Noël at two."

"I'd love that," I said, and then Aunt Clara was already pulling me away, muttering something about overly charming men.

"He's up to no good, you know."

I hoped so…

I was floating on clouds when I entered the shop, where Amber and Luca both were despite the late hour. I paused in the middle of the floor and spread my arms in declaration.

"I've met the man of my dreams. This spell has to come off right now."

Not waiting for their answer, I headed to my room. I had some serious daydreaming to do.

Five

I ARRIVED AT BREAKFAST BRIGHT AND early—for Sunday—despite a sleepless night. I'd been too excited to sleep.

I was too excited to have breakfast either, or too nervous, as if this were the first time I was going on a date. My mouth went a mile a minute as I described my evening, gushing about Jack, and it was a wonder that I managed to eat at all.

To my utter amazement, the rest of the household weren't at all excited and happy for me.

"I don't trust this," Giselle said, shaking her head. She was sitting at the head of the table, Griselda on her arms, petting the cat like a villain in a Bond movie.

Or maybe I was projecting.

I put down my fork. "Don't you start. Henry's cousin Ida already warned me that he's a womaniser. I know what I'm getting into. But I can't let this go. What if the spell is never broken? He's the only man who's not repulsed by me."

"And why is that?" Amber asked with a pointed look. "Are you sure he's not the one who put the spell on you?"

I pulled backwards in my chair as if she'd hit me. "Why would he have?" It hadn't even occurred to me. "He's gorgeous. I'd sooner believe he'd put a spell on himself to ward off over-eager women." I snickered at the idea. "And when would he have had time to cast it? We only met briefly in a café and Kane was affected by the spell moments later."

"A touch is enough with some spells, if it's been prepared in advance," Giselle said. Griselda squirmed in her arms, and she put her on the floor. As she straightened, she shot a scrutinising glance at me. "Did he touch you?"

"Well … we shook hands." I suddenly remembered the odd sensation when our hands met. I pressed my lips together stubbornly. "It wasn't him."

"There is a mage named Jack Palmer in London," Amber said, getting up and starting to clear the table.

"It's a perfectly normal English name," I argued. "And why would he spell me, even if he were the same man? I've never met him before. Do you think he went around London looking for a suitable subject to test the spell on?"

But they just shook their heads, unconvinced.

In a huff, I retired to my room to go through my wardrobe to choose the best look for my date. I wanted to look pretty, but not overeager or desperate, although I was both.

I only emerged an hour later to do my share of the household chores that were part of the rent. Sunday was cleaning day, and this week it was my turn to vacuum.

I hated vacuuming. I put all my anger at Amber's and Giselle's suspicions about Jack into it. I was in a much better mood when it was time to start preparing for my date.

Just how unconvinced the women of my household were of Jack's innocence became obvious when it was time for me to leave. Ashley was leaning against the hallway wall outside kitchen, and she straightened when she spotted me, looming over me.

"Amber said I have to come with you."

She was dressed in black jeans and T-shirt, her head cleanly shaven and gleaming. Since it was her day off, she'd added a row of rings to her ears and one eyebrow too, which she couldn't do at work. She looked like a fierce bodyguard, but I wasn't going to be intimidated into letting her accompany me.

"I don't need a chaperone," I growled, making her grin—probably because she found the sound funny.

"Relax. I'll just give you a lift. I won't come to the restaurant. I'll sit in the car and keep an eye on you from there."

As if that was better.

"And we're coming too," Amber added, emerging from the kitchen, "because Ashley doesn't know the mage families and might not recognise him."

Just my luck that this Sunday they didn't have chores to occupy themselves with like usually to keep them from meddling with my affairs.

Luca would probably have come too if he weren't dead to the world during the day.

It was no point arguing with them, so I just followed Ashley to her large Range Rover, practicing in my head the disdainful look I'd give them when they turned out to be wrong.

Brasserie Noël was a French restaurant in Soho, two streets north of Piccadilly Circus. The interior was from the 1930s, and the food was wonderful—and remarkably cheap for the quality and the location. There was a cabaret downstairs that put on shows every evening, though I'd never seen one.

I'd often had lunch there, as it was less than a mile from the gallery. The mere thought of their food made my mouth water during the three-mile drive across Central London.

The restaurant was on a small plaza diagonally to Piccadilly Theatre, and the closest place to park the car was by the theatre. By some luck—or magic?—Ashley snatched the last free spot there, with a good view over to the terrace of the restaurant that stretched on the plaza.

"Make sure you stay outside," Amber reminded me for the tenth time. The weather was beautiful, and I would have done it even without her telling me to, but I rolled my eyes.

"What do you think is going to happen? Even if he is the one who put the spell on me, he can't do anything funny in a public place."

Giselle's mouth pursed in displeasure. "There's something predatory in a man who would put a spell on a woman just because he can."

"Even a spell that's supposed to protect me from men?"

She nodded firmly. "Any spell done without your consent."

I couldn't exactly argue with that.

"Maybe he won't show up if he's such a horrible man," I said, miffed, but the mere thought made my guts twist in disappointment. I wanted to see him again.

Saved by the Spell

"If he doesn't show up, we'll come and have lunch with you so that you won't be embarrassed," Ashley promised. "Their food smells delicious."

I didn't ask how she could detect it all the way here—werewolf nose—and just exited the car.

I was dressed in my new jeans again—they really did make my bottom look great—but the top under the blazer was sleeveless and it had a plunging neckline that gave me good cleavage. I tugged my clothes in place and closed the door.

Amber lowered the window on her side. "I'll text you if I recognise him and think you should leave."

"I will not bail out on a date!"

"Of course not," Ashley said with a grin. "It would be a waste of good food."

That brought a smile to my face as I crossed the street to the plaza.

The terrace was almost full, but I could instantly see that Jack hadn't arrived yet. Undeterred, I peeked inside the restaurant, but he wasn't there either. I wasn't discouraged—I'd been overly punctual—and just took the only available table left on the terrace.

A waiter materialised next to me almost instantly, affecting a French accent even though he was perfectly English. It was difficult to say whether his snooty attitude was French too, or caused by the spell. Probably a bit of both.

"Is mademoiselle ready to order or will she wait for others?" he asked even as he handed me the menu.

"I'll wait."

My phone pinged just then with a message from Ashley, with a screengrab of the menu: Order me this to go!

"Do you do take-away too?" I asked the waiter, who assured me they did, so I placed the order. There were no additional orders from Amber and Giselle. Their loss.

Before the waiter could return with a pitcher of water, I spotted Jack sauntering down the pedestrian court from the direction of Piccadilly Circus. My heart began to beat faster, and I had to take hold of my chair so that I wouldn't jump up to wave at him.

He spotted me and a smile spread on his face. He hurried his steps and was soon taking a seat next to me. "I'm sorry I'm late," he said, placing a kiss on my cheek.

Completely breathless, I fought to find my composure. He was not my first date, for heaven's sake.

"I just arrived myself," I assured him, but the effect was instantly ruined by the waiter, who returned to inquire if I wanted the take-away box immediately or later.

Jack's brows shot up. "You thought I wouldn't show up?"

I had to grin, he looked so dismayed. "No, my housemate heard I'd be coming here, and she made me order food to go for her."

I told the waiter later would do, and by the time I turned my attention back to Jack, he was sitting more relaxed in his chair. I'd deliberately left him the one that faced the car. Just because I didn't believe he was guilty didn't mean I'd make the others' job more difficult for them.

My phone pinged, but I ignored it. I didn't care if Amber and Giselle had recognised Jack. I would not leave. And if they wanted food, they'd just have to order directly.

We placed our orders and Jack leaned back in his chair, one arm thrown over the backrest. "This was a great idea."

Saved by the Spell

I wholeheartedly agreed. "Do you come here often?"

"At least once a week. It's near my office." He'd told me the previous night that he worked as a private asset manager in a banking firm not far from the gallery.

"And the café where we met?"

His smile turned into an apologetic grimace. "Actually, I kind of followed you there."

"Oh?"

My heart began to beat so fast I feared it would come out of my chest, but I couldn't tell whether it was for excitement or dismay.

"I spotted you outside the Tube station and I thought you were really beautiful." He lowered his unique eyes slowly down my body and back to my face, and they lit with an appreciative gleam. "And may I say, you're looking wonderful today too."

I pressed my head down to hide my blush.

"Anyway, I thought I'd just see where you were going, maybe ask you out, but then I sort of lost my nerve, and I had to follow you in the café."

He didn't seem like the kind of man who wouldn't know how to ask a girl out, but I nodded. "And then we met by chance again yesterday."

"I was actually prepared to haunt the café every day if needed until I spotted you again," he said with a self-deprecating laugh that I found endearing.

"Why didn't you come to the gallery?"

His brows shot up, his face a picture of bafflement. "That didn't even occur to me."

We burst out laughing.

We had a wonderful lunch. And I have no idea what I ate. It was so effortless to talk with him. I was sorry when it came to an end. He insisted on paying, but since I had to pay for Ashley's lunch anyway, I declined.

"I have to see you again," he said in a serious tone as we were standing outside the terrace, preparing to go to separate directions.

"I'd love that."

He leaned down to briefly kiss me. His lips were soft and warm, and tasted slightly of the wine he'd had with lunch. My bones turned to liquid.

"I'll call you."

"You'd better or I'll put a hex on you," I said, breathless, and he burst out laughing.

I waited for him to disappear around a bend in the street before hurrying to the car that had waited the whole time. Ashley had switched seats with Amber so she wouldn't have to drive, and she snatched the food container from my hands.

"I'm starving." She began to wolf down the food—pun intended—and I climbed into the back seat.

Amber gave me a stern look from behind the wheel. "Why didn't you leave when I told you to?"

I crossed my arms over my chest. "Because I didn't want to. He's utterly charming and there was nothing to worry about."

"But that was Jack Palmer," Giselle said in a patient tone.

"I know." I'd told them his name myself.

"Jack is one of the best mages of his generation. And even though he hasn't made his intentions public, he's likely to challenge Archibald for the leadership of our order."

Colour drained from my face and the wonderful food threatened to push up. "What do you mean?"

Saved by the Spell

"That I figured out the motivation for your spell. If he wants to challenge Archibald, it will suit him perfectly to unsettle him first."

I stared at them in dismay, and Giselle gave me a commiserating look.

"I think it definitely was Jack who put the spell on you."

Six

"We'll have to speak with Archibald," Amber stated, turning the car towards Belgravia, about two miles from Soho.

"What difference does it make?" I pleaded, suddenly embarrassed to face my boss. "If Jack wants me to unsettle Kane, shouldn't I stay away?"

But they were adamant.

I was fighting tears the whole drive. I refused to believe Jack would have deliberately put a spell on me. He couldn't have kissed me like that if he had. There had to be another explanation.

"Maybe someone else who wants to challenge Kane is only using him," I tried, but a wall of silence made me retreat to my corner of the car.

They'd see I was right.

Kane lived in the Mews behind Eaton Court, an immensely popular location in an insanely expensive part of Central London, south of Hyde Park. Aristocrats used to keep their horses and grooms in the Mews between the Georgian terraces where they'd lived. They formed rows of flat two-storey terraces on both sides of a gated courtyard, with garages below and the living quarters above.

I was dragging my feet as we made our way to his front door. I didn't want to be here. I didn't want Kane to learn that I'd—possibly—been foolish. "Maybe he's at the gallery."

It wasn't open on Sundays, but he often spent time there at odd hours. But his Jag was parked sideways in front of his two-bay garage, banishing that hope.

"What if he has a lady friend there?" I suggested hastily when Amber reached to ring the doorbell. "He wouldn't want me to witness it."

She shot me an amused glare as she pressed the buzzer. "He's a grown man and gets to take whoever he wants to bed. We don't need to know or care."

"I'd like to know…" Ashley muttered, and I kind of agreed with her.

The thought distracted me, and before I realised it, Kane was answering the door.

He didn't look like a man who'd just climbed out of bed, although the jogging bottoms and T-shirt were exactly the kind of clothes you pulled hastily on when the doorbell rang. And his hair was messier than normal.

I stared at him with my mouth open. I could count with fingers of one hand how often I'd seen him in clothes other than a suit—not including the one time I'd seen him almost naked, which … wow. I'd been absolutely convinced he dressed formally even at home.

His brows shot up when he saw the four of us. "This is a pleasant surprise," he said politely. "Emphasis on surprise."

"We need to talk," Giselle informed him. "We think we know who put the spell on Phoebe and why."

Saved by the Spell

Wordlessly, he stepped aside to let us in.

We climbed the stairs to an open living room and kitchen; the bedroom and the bathroom were behind the kitchen. The space was beautifully furnished in mid-century modern, with books and art everywhere.

I spotted the hideous lamp Kane had acquired for the auction. It fit the room amazingly well, and didn't even look so ugly here.

"You bought the lamp," I noted aloud to buy time. He smiled, pleased.

"We reached an agreement with the owner about the price."

He waved a hand at a seating group, a sofa and three armchairs upholstered in off-white around a low coffee table. I had bad memories of the table, as I'd found him bound to it by a demon.

His memories were probably worse.

I sank heavily on the sofa with Giselle next to me. "I think you should tell him," she said to me.

I looked at Kane, who sat as far away from me as possible, fighting to keep his composure—and I burst out crying.

I surprised everyone, including myself. I couldn't remember the last time I'd cried like this. Not even my breakup with Troy had made me anything but furious.

I buried my face in my hands and Giselle wrapped a consoling arm around me. Kane shot up. "I'll go make tea."

"I'll help," Ashley declared, getting up too. She was followed by Amber.

"Me too."

I'd stopped crying by the time the three of them set the tea tray on the table in front of me. I wiped my eyes into a handkerchief Kane gave me—a proper muslin one—and pulled myself together. Giselle gave me a cup of tea.

"I'm sorry," I said, taking a sip. "I don't know what came over me."

"It has been a stressful week, what with the spell making your life difficult," Kane consoled me, but I shook my head.

"It's more that I was given a glimpse of what my life could be without it, and then it turned out to be a lie."

He leaned forwards in his armchair, only to pull hastily back. "Just tell me."

I heaved a deep sigh. "Yesterday, at the engagement party, I met the most charming man."

The scene kept playing in my head, vividly. Nothing in my memory of it indicated that Jack hadn't been in earnest. Kane's jaw worked, as if he wanted to say something, but he nodded, so I continued:

"He was interested in me too. And he wasn't repulsed by me. The spell didn't work on him."

His eyes sharpened. "How is that possible?"

"Giselle and Amber say it's because he was the one who cast the spell." I still couldn't believe it. "I just don't understand why."

"It was Jack Palmer," Amber explained for me. "This could be his way to challenge you for the leadership."

He pulled straight. "By casting a spell on my human employee?" I tried not to wince for being called human, as it made clear that the rest of them weren't. "That is not acceptable."

Amber began to pour another round of tea, even though only she and Ashley had emptied their cups. "It's the only explanation that makes sense. And it's a rather

Saved by the Spell

good challenge too. It would definitely show your skill if you can break it—or his if you can't."

He didn't look convinced. "How would he even know about Phoebe to attack her?"

"He said he'd spotted me outside the Tube station, but I think that was a lie." I felt sick, and I put the cup away. "I think he's been keeping an eye on the gallery, and he seized the opportunity when he saw me to go in the café."

"Maybe…" Kane frowned. "But why didn't he cast the spell on Mrs Walsh? She's easier to access in the gallery, and it would hurt my business more if she weren't able to serve the customers."

I rubbed my face as I tried to come up with an explanation for Jack's actions. "Maybe he intended to demonstrate that he wasn't affected by the spell by dating me. He couldn't do that with Mrs Walsh, because she's married." And twenty-five years older than him, so probably not as appealing an option. "And you might not have noticed it so soon, if he had used her."

"Are the reasons important anyway?" Ashley pitched in. "The fact remains that your employee is highly inconvenienced by his spell and will remain so if you don't find a way to break it."

Kane nodded. "That'll have to be my priority."

"I'll help," I stated, determination pushing away my upset. "You've had a whole week and you haven't found the spell yet."

His face turned forbidding. "I can't let you in the library of our headquarters."

I gave him a slow look. We'd been through his reluctance to let me participate before when I was cursed.

61

I wasn't about to let him push me to the side-line when it concerned me.

"Why not? It's not like I don't know you people exist, and I've been to your headquarters already."

"We'll all go," Giselle said. "We need all eyes on the job."

Wisely enough, Kane didn't argue further and just went to change his clothes. The jeans and dark green V-neck cashmere jumper were almost as odd as the joggers had been, but they fit his tall and leanly muscled body perfectly. Much better than the suit.

Ashley's car was large enough to fit us all, so we took it. The mage council's headquarters were in Thames Ditton, on the south side of the Thames from Hampton Court, about thirteen miles upriver from where Kane lived. Sunday traffic there and back was surprisingly heavy, the fine weather luring people to the parks, so we settled in for a slow and aggravating ride.

"This has really upset you, Phoebe," Kane noted when we had cleared the worst congestion and crossed the river in Chelsea. He was sitting in the front, mostly so he didn't have to be near me. He tried to hide it, but it put a strain on him to be so close to me for such a long time.

His question threatened to make the tears spill again. "I don't understand why he had to pretend to be attracted to me, if he was the one who spelled me." I wiped my cheeks with the back of my hand. "Why didn't he simply wait to see what you would do?"

"He could truly be attracted to you," he suggested in a kind tone.

I crossed my arms over my chest, hugging myself. "Then why the spell? He doesn't need it to charm women."

Saved by the Spell

"It's not a charm spell. Those don't exist," he explained. I shook my head, because I hadn't meant that.

"It keeps the competition away really effectively, and makes a woman truly grateful that anyone is paying attention to her."

I'd practically crawled into his arms.

He tilted his head in acknowledgement. "I'm really sorry you were caught in this business again."

I was too, but it was hardly his fault. "Maybe it's a compliment to you. They're not brave enough to attack you directly."

The notion clearly pleased him, but he brushed it away with a wave of his hand. "I think this is part of a wider attack to undermine me. With Jack distracting me, someone else has a chance to make their move."

"You mean Jack's not your challenger?" Amber asked, leaning closer to hear him, as she was sitting directly behind him. He made to shake his head, then hesitated.

"The rules specifically state that the attack has to be on the leader, so this doesn't count. He may challenge me later, but for now I think he's helping someone else."

"So, who do you think he's teamed with?"

He rubbed the bridge of his nose as he gave her question a thought. "We still don't know who the mastermind behind that secret society was that frightened even Danielle. Maybe it's him."

Silence fell in the car. Danielle had been terrified of him—and she was dating a warlock.

"I think we'd best to prepare for worst," Amber declared. "You should keep an eye out for an attack from this unknown—or other challengers—while the rest of us look for the spell."

"I'll stay with Kane," Ashley said, slowing down to turn at an intersection. "I'm not much for books, but I can keep him alive."

Kane paled a little. "Surely you don't think they'd threaten my life?"

We jumped as she blared the horn to make the car in front of us move faster, as if she was behind the wheel of a fire engine. "Best be prepared for everything."

We reached the mage council's headquarters eventually. It was a large, rectangular, brown-brick with a façade from the Georgian era, though the original building was much older; some buildings in the village dated from the Middle Ages. It shared a car park with a large Queen Anne style manor that functioned as an expensive care home for the elderly.

The last time I was here, it had been night and I hadn't been able to see much. I looked around curiously, admiring the neat, verdant lawn between the car park and the river, and the beautiful buildings. There were more people around too, with orderlies pushing residents of the care home in wheelchairs on the footpath by the river, and visitors driving in and out from the car park.

It was a beautiful September day, but I suddenly shivered with cold. Kane placed a hand on my shoulder, and I appreciated the gesture, as it clearly cost him. His arm was stiff, and he wouldn't stand close.

"We'll find the counter-spell. Don't worry."

"I know. It's not the spell that gets to me as much as the betrayal. Which is funny, considering I only met Jack yesterday. Well, Monday, but that was brief."

"He deliberately used you. Of course that hurts."

I couldn't tell him how utterly smitten I'd been with Jack after such a short acquaintance. I'd already imagined

Saved by the Spell

telling my parents that I'd found someone I'd spend the rest of my life with and that they could start planning an April wedding.

Such a fool.

The façade of the mages' headquarters consisted of tall French doors. Afternoon sun slanted through the many panes into the entrance hall, making the polished tile floor gleam. There wasn't a speck of dust in sight. There weren't people around either, and it was eerily silent.

The library was on the right side of the hall from the door, taking the entire shorter end of the building. It was a square room with no windows, and it seemed gloomy in the artificial light after the sunshine. Tall shelves covered every available space, and they were full of books, old and new. I drew a deep breath, enjoying the scent of books.

"I didn't realise there were so many spell books in the world," I said with awe.

"These aren't only spell books," Kane explained. "But there are a lot of those too."

"So where should we start?"

"I've been going through the older books, as it is a medieval spell. I think I'll continue with those. You should go through the modern ones, in case it's reproduced in one of them."

"Surely we would've heard about it in that case," Giselle noted.

"Maybe, but we can't overlook the possibility."

He and Amber went to the older books, and I followed Giselle to the newer ones. Ashley settled at the open door to the entrance hall to keep watch.

For all that I was into arts and antiques, old books had never been my passion, so I didn't mind that we'd been put to study the newer ones—though they weren't exactly modern either but from the late nineteenth century onwards.

"Shall we try to deduce the likeliest books to contain the spell, or go through all of them?" I asked Giselle who eyed the shelf in front of us in dismay.

"I can't decide. Part of me knows that a spell like this is a highly specialised one and will be in a particular book, but I don't want to overlook anything."

"We'll check them all, then."

At least the modern books had tables of content and indexes. It made the task much easier. One by one, both took a book, opened it, checked the pertinent parts, were disappointed, and put the book back. After an hour of that, my arms were starting to ache, and I was parched.

"Any chance for tea?" I asked Giselle, who perked.

"Absolutely."

She practically fled the room, leaving me to handle our lot alone, but that was fine. I needed tea more than I needed company. But there had to be a better way to approach this.

"Can people loan these out?" I asked loud enough so that Kane and Amber could hear me where they were at the other end. Maybe there was a register we could check.

"Only with permission, from me," Kane said. "Which I haven't given anyone lately. And the room is warded so that no one can remove the books without my say-so."

I worried my lips with my teeth as I tried to come up with other possibilities. "Wouldn't it show the mage's skill if they could smuggle a book out anyway? And would that be an acceptable attack on you?"

Kane and Amber shared a look. "Yes…"

Saved by the Spell

"So maybe you should check if anyone has removed your wards?"

Kane grimaced. Pivoting around, he marched out of the library, and we followed curiously. He faced the library door and made a series of gestures with his hands. Nothing happened.

"Well, fuck," he said, stunning me. I hadn't often heard him curse. "The wards are gone."

"And that would mean…"

"That there's no point for us to go through the library. Jack has stolen the book."

Seven

WE RETREATED TO THE DINING ROOM on the other side of the hall, where Giselle set the tea at one end of the long table. I sank gratefully on a chair and took a long sip of the cup she placed in front of me.

Kane sat at the head of the table, his back turned to us, and stared out of the open double doors towards the library, slowly sipping his tea. It didn't seem to make him feel better—and it was excellent tea.

I'd worked for him long enough to recognise the mood. "It's not your fault that the wards were taken down."

His jaw worked as he controlled his anger at himself. "I should've checked them more regularly. I've been here every day this past week, and it didn't even occur to me to look."

I could understand how that was aggravating.

"You're a nice person who trusts people."

He only grunted in answer. I wasn't discouraged; I'd have quit the first month if his moods upset me. And I wouldn't have been much of an assistant if I didn't have helpful suggestions to make.

"Now that you know the book is taken, maybe you could do a tracking spell to locate it?"

Giselle had done a spell to track where the curse statuette had been sent from and I thought they could do one here. But Kane shook his head.

"We would need to know which book was taken, and even then it wouldn't work without a connection to it."

I put my cup down with a frustrated clank that made the contents slosh. "What use is magic if it can't detect the simplest things?"

He gave me a sideways smile. "It has its uses, but it can't do the impossible." He paused, pursed his lips in deep thought. "Although, there is actually something we could try…"

He shot up and marched out of the dining room.

"Thanks, it's not like I wanted to know what it is," I shouted after him, annoyed. Ashley grinned.

"Mages, huh."

"Shouldn't you be going after him?"

She jumped up, sending her chair flying backwards. "I'm new to this bodyguard thing."

I fetched her chair and righted it. "Well, you managed to handle the demon Dufort sent after him, so I'm sure you can handle anything."

She grinned, but before she could follow Kane, he returned and glared at Amber and Giselle. "Are you coming?"

Baffled, the women put their teacups down and rose from the table. "What do you need us for?" Amber asked.

"We need to perform the time-wheel spell, and I need you two for it."

Saved by the Spell

Amber was instantly intrigued. "You want to see who took down the wards?"

"Yes. But if I do it by myself, I'll only be able to reach back a week or so. We'll have to assume that the book has been gone for longer than that."

"Do you need us?" I asked, ready to follow them, but he lifted a hand to stop me.

"No. Best if you wait here."

"But I want to see…"

He frowned. "Fine, but stay out of the way and do not interrupt no matter what happens. Everyone who has been here will appear as apparitions and walk through you, which can be unnerving."

Ashley and I finished our tea while the mages prepared for the spell. It seemed to take forever and require many ingredients, which Giselle fetched from somewhere deeper in the house, running up and down past us.

I followed their progress with great curiosity from my seat at the dining room table, the open double doors offering a good view. Amber and Kane drew intricate patterns on the tile floor with chalk, following instructions from a book Kane was holding. By the time they were finished, it covered most of the entrance hall floor.

This was clearly a massive spell.

"Okay, we're ready to start," Kane said, putting the book away. He pointed to a corner farthest from the library door. "You can sit there. No one has likely been there during this time, so no apparitions should go through you."

Ashley and I obeyed eagerly. We skipped over the chalk lines and sat on the floor at the appointed place. I was starting to feel nervous. I wanted to squeeze Ashley's hand like a little girl, but I kept my hands to myself, fearing that a cool werewolf would scoff at it.

And then she took my hand and squeezed it tightly. "Just so you don't do anything stupid."

Giselle, Amber and Kane took their places on the pattern. They concentrated briefly, and then began to chant. Amber lit the candles with magic one by one, while Giselle scattered the spell ingredients on the floor a pinch at a time, seemingly at random. Some of them burst in fire, some began to smoke, some just lay there. Kane made complicated movements with his arms, twisting them together and opening again, looking like an enthusiastic orchestra conductor about to take flight.

I didn't understand the words, but their voices grew steadily as they went on. A power began to press on my chest, making it difficult to breathe. The door out rattled as if wind were shaking it. A howling rose, covering the chanting voices, only to cut abruptly.

Darkness fell.

I made to shoot up, only to be stopped by Ashley's unyielding hand holding mine. I guess she had been right to detain me in advance.

I couldn't see anything, not even myself, which was truly frightening, as if I weren't even there. The silence was eerie, and I shivered.

Forms began to materialise in the darkness, translucent human figures lit by some inner light that made them glow yellow. They walked backwards, as if time was reversing.

I recognised us, scurrying across the hall this way and that, the pace picking up as the spell advanced. Distant, wan light ebbed and flowed, never properly illuminating the space, marking the passing of days.

Saved by the Spell

Kane walked backwards into the library, only to reappear a moment later, backwards again. This repeated several times. New faces showed up, but not as many as I would have imagined. Apparently, the mages didn't need to visit the headquarters all that often. A cleaning lady made her rounds, mopping the hall, poking through us with her transparent mop as she cleaned the corner, her backward movements almost like a dance.

There were a couple of occasions when several people went through the hall to the dining room. I presumed they were the council heading to their weekly meeting. Kane and Amber were among them.

Only Kane visited the library. No one tried to break the wards.

The forms were starting to become fainter, their faces more difficult to discern. As if from a distance, I heard Kane bellow, and I felt a pressure rise until it seemed to be crushing my bones. But it worked. The forms turned clear again, moving at a faster pace.

To my surprise, I appeared again with the same people I was here with today, plus Luca and Danielle. It was the night we were here to break the curse. We'd gone backwards over a month in time, and still no one had taken down the wards at the library door.

Finally, when the spell had reached what I estimated was a week before my previous visit, Jack appeared. My breathing caught, mostly for disappointment. I hadn't wanted him to be here.

Since the timeline went backwards, he backed into the library with a book under his arm, only to exit a moment later without it and stand in front of the library doors.

And this time he wasn't alone.

There was a cloaked figure next to him. A hood covered their face, and the shape of the cloak made it difficult to tell if it was a man or a woman. They stood slightly stooped, so their height was difficult to discern too, but likely as tall as Jack.

Together they unravelled the wards. Or since it happened backwards, recast them. I strained my eyes, trying to identify the other person, but before I could, the time-wheel spell abruptly ended. Light returned and I could see again. The three mages where still on their spots, slowly lowering their arms.

Their shoulders slumped in exhaustion and sweat shone on their foreheads. They stepped out of their places and looked at each other, pleased. Ashley let go of my hand and I rubbed it to get the blood flowing again. She'd really squeezed it hard.

She helped me up. "It was definitely Jack," I said, sounding disappointed even though we'd known it already. "Who was the cloaked one?"

Kane shook his head, looking grim. "No idea."

"That's not good."

"Not in the slightest," he said dryly. Then he sighed. "The wards were taken down weeks ago."

I nodded. "When you were on holiday. They made sure you wouldn't be here to notice it."

His face was grim. "They've had time to plan this well, and we have no idea what's going on."

"We know that they want you removed from your office."

"But with this much ... malice..." He grimaced. "I was under the impression that I've been doing a good job as the leader. I've certainly heard no complaints. A

Saved by the Spell

challenge is expected, but this..." His voice drifted away and he shook his head, amazed.

I reached my hand to pat him on the arm, but then I realised it would only make him feel worse and let my hand drop.

"It's probably not personal," I settled with. "They want power and you're in their way."

"I guess." He sighed. "I'd best restore these wards."

While he handled that, the rest of us cleaned the chalk markings off the floor. My thoughts were on Jack and his betrayal, and the mystery person.

It was dark by the time everything was clean, the wards were back, and the building was locked up. Exhaustion slowed our steps as we made our way to the car. My stomach growled, reminding me that I'd only had a cup of tea since lunch.

The care home had quieted down for the evening, but there were still a couple of cars in the car park. Ashley triggered the locks of her car remotely and its lights flashed briefly, blinding us.

That's when the attack happened.

~ ~ ~

I'D NOTICED THE WOMAN approaching our car, but I hadn't paid any attention to her, assuming she was a visitor to the care home. I came to regret my negligence when she immobilised us with a wave of her hand.

Correction, she immobilised me and Ashley. Giselle and Amber had been entering the car and managed to avoid the hit. Kane was able to react in time, triggering some sort of shield which kept his hands free.

A mage didn't need anything else.

Frozen on the spot, I could only watch as the two mages began to sling spells at each other. Colourful lights were flashing, wind twirled around them, and weird smells reached my nose, cloying and burning at the same time.

They seemed to be equal in skills, but the woman had the advantage, as she could move around freely. But she couldn't attack Kane from behind, because she'd immobilised him against the car.

She was about fifty and stocky, with a stern face, and brown hair in a neat, no-nonsense bob. She wore a tweed skirt suit and sturdy leather walking shoes: a woman who walked ten miles across the moors before breakfast with her wolfhounds.

Kane was younger and in great shape, but he was already exhausted from the time-wheel spell. I feared he wouldn't be able to keep up.

"Can't you do anything?" I asked Amber, who had climbed out of the car to watch.

"No. She's Cynthia Griffin, a member of the council. This is a legitimate leadership challenge. He'll lose if we interfere."

"But what if outsiders notice?"

"I've shrouded us. Technically, Cynthia should've done that before she attacked, but I guess she forgot."

"Or feared that it would tire her too much and left it out deliberately," Giselle noted dryly. Then she raised her voice. "It's not cool to cheat, Cynthia!"

The woman glanced at her briefly, and it was all Kane needed to free his legs from her binding spell. Now he had better range and could launch proper attacks. The colours of his attacks became brighter, and Amber and Giselle made impressed sounds.

Saved by the Spell

Cynthia was soon in retreat, falling back across the lawn towards the river, with Kane pressing on. I don't know where he found the energy, but with the next attack he immobilized her.

That freed me. The sudden change made me stumble and I almost fell on my face. Giselle managed to grab a hold of me at the last moment.

"Thanks."

We gathered around Kane and Cynthia. She looked put-out rather than angry. Kane faced her, breathing heavily but otherwise calm.

"In front of these witnesses, you challenged me for the leadership of the council of mages, yes?" he asked. Cynthia had the use of her head and she nodded.

"Yes." Her voice was calm.

"In front of these witnesses, your challenge was accepted, yes?"

She nodded again, pursing her lips. "Yes."

"And in front of these witnesses, I won and you lost, yes?"

"Yes," she said firmly.

"And as I free you, you agree not to challenge me again during this cycle?"

"I agree."

Kane gestured with his hand and the woman was freed. He offered her his hand and they shook.

"Good battle," she said, pleased. "I thought I had you there for a moment."

Kane bowed. "You almost did. But if you'd handled the shroud yourself as you should've, I would've won faster."

She grimaced. "I completely forgot it." She nodded at Amber. "Thank you."

Amber nodded in acknowledgement.

Kane wasn't done with her. "Now, I have to ask, were you acting alone?"

Cynthia pulled back. "Of course I was. What a strange question."

"We have a reason to suspect that Jack Palmer is helping the challenge of someone by creating distractions for me."

Her lip curled in distaste. "I wouldn't team with that impertinent boy if he paid me."

"Good." Kane's tone suggested he had never expected otherwise. "Suppose you don't know who it might be he's helping?"

"I haven't really paid attention to what he does, but I'll let you know if I hear anything." With that, she nodded at Kane, headed to her car, and drove away.

The moment her taillights disappeared, Kane's legs gave up and he collapsed heavily on the lawn. As a group, we surged to help him, but Ashley halted us with a growl. She leaned down and lifted him into her arms as if he weighed nothing.

"Come on, let's get you in the car."

He wasn't quite out of it, but he didn't seem to be able to move on his own, so she manoeuvred him deftly into the front seat.

"I shouldn't have battled right after the time-wheel spell," he managed to say.

"As if you had a choice," Amber reminded him. "You know the rules better than anyone. The challenge has to be accepted immediately."

By the time we reached Kane's home, he'd recovered enough to walk in by himself. We followed in case he collapsed again.

Saved by the Spell

"You'd best head to bed," Giselle ordered. "I'll make you my special tea."

I'd had her special tea and knew it made you sleep in no time. Soon enough, he was snoring in his bedroom. Maybe literally. I wasn't brave enough to go and check.

Before we left, Amber fortified the wards on Kane's door to keep him safe. He wouldn't be able to handle another attack tonight. Then we headed home too. It had been a long day and I needed sleep.

I should have guessed I wouldn't be given the chance.

Eight

AUNT CLARA WAS SITTING ON THE RED velvet sofa in our living room, drinking tea from Giselle's Royal Doulton cup from 1920s she'd inherited from her aunt with the house. Luca sat in an armchair opposite her—sans tea—his eyes glazing over as he listened to her stories of how her bones had predicted doom. She was currently in the energy crisis of the 70s.

Pity he looked my age and couldn't admit he'd lived through it.

He spotted us and surged up. "There you are. I tried to call you but your phone had died."

We'd all switched them off for the time-wheel spell. Apparently, none of us had remembered to switch them back on.

"Sorry about that. We went book hunting with my boss."

I hoped my aunt thought it was for the gallery. Luca retreated hastily to the kitchen, and I can't say I blamed him. Aunt Clara could be exhausting.

I gave her a questioning smile. "What brings you here, at this hour?"

Not that it was late; it just felt that way.

She put her teacup down on the sofa table and gave a longsuffering sigh. "It's this awful business with Olivia."

I sat on the armchair Luca had vacated, utterly puzzled. "What awful business? The engagement? I thought you were pleased about it."

Her mouth pursed as if she were sucking lemons. "Well, I'm not. There's something distasteful about the hastiness of it. If she's not pregnant—and she insists she isn't—then why the hurry? My bones are predicting doom, and you'll have to find out why."

I had no idea what to say, but knowing her I couldn't just brush her notions aside. "Surely a lawyer would be better suited for the job?" Or a private investigator.

She lifted a hand, warding off my suggestion. "No, I don't trust outsiders. You'll have to do it. And if everything isn't as it should, I want you to make Olivia call off the engagement."

I pulled back, dismayed. "Absolutely not."

"Even if it would ruin her life?" she demanded, but I held my ground.

"Even then. She's a grown woman and can make her own mistakes."

Her nostrils flared. "We'll see about that. In the meantime, find out what you can."

She pulled herself up and sailed out of the room, nodding regally at Amber and Giselle in parting. Luca hurried after her to see her out. I should have done that, but I was suddenly too exhausted to care.

"Well, that was something else," Ashley noted from where she was sitting at the dining table, eating cold stew straight from the container. "How are you going to find out what's going on?"

Saved by the Spell

I let my head drop against the backrest. "I have no idea. I didn't really get to know anyone at the party last night." I'd been too busy being charmed by Jack and repulsing the rest. "I guess I could call Henry's cousin, Ida."

"Or you could ask Jack," Amber suggested, and I shuddered in horror.

"Absolutely not. I don't want anything to do with him."

Fool me once, and so forth.

"You can't cut him off yet. He'll realise that you know he's behind the spell if you suddenly ghost him."

Giselle brought me tea and I took a grateful sip, though I was eyeing the cold stew with envy. She sat next to me. "Moreover, he has the book, and we need it back if we want to break the spell."

"I can't just ask him if he has it," I protested.

"You're an antiques dealer. You can ask if he has old books lying about," she suggested, and Amber nodded.

"Get yourself invited to his home and snoop around."

That was an annoyingly sensible suggestion.

"Fine. But I won't enjoy it."

~ ~ ~

I TOOK THE EASY WAY OUT the next morning. I sent a message to Olivia asking for Ida's phone number. She called me back when I was walking from the Tube station to the gallery.

"I'm so glad you liked Ida," she gushed. "She's great. I don't actually have her number, but I'll ask Harry." She paused and her voice turned coy when she continued: "So … I hear you went out with Jack yesterday?"

My stomach fell. "Yes, we had lunch."

"Tell me everything."

"It was lunch. Not much to tell."

"Oh, come on. Surely there's more than that?"

I racked my mind for a suitable explanation for my unenthusiastic response. "Ida said he's a womaniser. I only recently got rid of one. I don't need another."

"Surely he's not that bad? Give him another chance. He's the best man and you're my maid of honour. You'll have to get along."

I almost dropped the phone hearing I'd been promoted from bridesmaid to maid of honour. It promised to be a wedding out of hell if I didn't get rid of the spell by then. "I'll see what I can do." I drew a fortifying breath. "Before I forget, your grandmother is on the warpath. She's decided there's something iffy about your engagement."

She groaned. "Not her too. Dad's already threatening to have his lawyers check the family. What could they possibly have against Harry?"

"There's no harm in making sure. Just let him check. He'll do it anyway." I couldn't believe I was siding with Aunt Clara after all, but if Olivia's father was already on it, I didn't have to get involved.

"Fine, but I retain the right to gloat when his suspicions turn out to be baseless."

"That's the best part."

I'd reached the gallery by the time we ended the call. I glanced at the café across the court and a sour taste rose to my mouth. Could I ever go to that place again? I'd miss their blueberry muffins, but I didn't want to be reminded of Jack. Or run into him there.

As I sat at my desk, I realised that I hadn't felt like I was being observed in the Tube this morning like I had

Saved by the Spell

almost every morning the past week. Or had I been too preoccupied to pay attention?

Would it be too much to hope that whatever it had been had gone away?

Maybe it had been Cynthia keeping an eye on me in case I was the weak link to Kane, like everyone seemed to think. I decided to ask him if it was possible to keep tabs on someone with magic the moment he arrived.

Only he didn't.

Arrive to work, that is. I had his tea ready at nine, and was sitting behind my desk dabbling with this and that as I waited for him. At ten past nine, I checked my watch to see if it had died—or was advancing. At twenty past nine, I checked my messages for the third time, in case he had informed me of a change in his plans.

He hadn't.

His tea had turned cold by half past nine and I threw it away. I was debating whether to make a new pot when my phone pinged with a message. The speed with which I rushed to my desk to check it belied my worry.

But it wasn't from him. Olivia had sent me Ida's phone number with a wish that we'd become great friends. Since I wasn't great friends with Olivia, I didn't see why I'd have to befriend Ida. But I had liked her and I needed her help with Jack, so I sent her a message and asked if we could meet for lunch.

After a brief hesitation, I sent a message to Kane too. This wasn't the first time he didn't show up at work in the morning, and it was always because he'd gone to check a promising piece of antique someone had offered for him. He didn't always remember to inform me about it.

But what if I was wrong? He had been attacked last night, and had been in poor shape when we left him. What if he was still in bed, too weak to get up?

What if he'd been attacked again!

I started to worry in earnest, the pit in my stomach growing steadily as the morning advanced and he didn't answer my messages and calls. I had a ton of work to do for the auction, but I found it difficult to concentrate.

Should I go check him at home? But if he was under attack, what could I do?

Pity Ashley was on duty or I'd send her there.

When a message from Ida arrived, agreeing to lunch, I considered calling it off after all. But I needed to learn more about Jack, and I wanted the spell lifted off. So I just left a message to Kane on his desk, took my bag, and went to meet her.

I didn't have far to go. The pedestrian court opened into a small plaza fifty yards from the gallery, with restaurants practically in every building. It was a beautiful and fashionable place to have lunch, and almost every table was full on the terraces lining the plaza.

I spotted Ida outside a corner pub at the far end, seated already. She waved at me when she spotted me.

"I claimed a table for us. Go order our food. I'll have whatever salad they have, and water."

I did as I was told. The queue at the bar was shorter than I expected, and the barkeep was a woman, so there were no delays due to disgust, and I was soon back at the table.

"I was surprised by your message," Ida said. She was wearing a suit today, and the masculine cut suited her tall frame. With the geometrically cut shock-red hair, she looked striking. "And surprised to learn that you work so close to where I do."

I took a seat and smiled. "Where do you work?"

"I'm an accountant at Nationwide, not far from here."

"You don't look like an accountant," I blurted, and she laughed.

"I get that a lot."

"Do you live in this part of town too?" I wasn't that curious, but thanks to my mom, small talk came automatically to me.

She made a face. "God no. Can anybody afford that?" Since I'd recently faced that question, I tilted my head in wry acknowledgement. "I live in Bushwood, and even that is a bit steep for me. But at least it's green and I can take the Circle Line all the way to work."

I perked. "I use the Circle Line too! Imagine we've never run into each other there."

"We probably have, but who pays attention to people in the Tube." She paused and gave me a curious look. "So I guess you want to know more about Jack?"

Her direct approach threw me, but since that's why I was here, I nodded. "We had lunch yesterday, but I want to know more about him before I go any farther with a womaniser."

"You want to know if he's worth the broken heart?" she guessed, and I grinned.

"He'd have to be pretty spectacular for that."

She barked another laugh. "No man is that spectacular."

"Amen to that."

The waiter arrived with our food. He flashed a flirtatious smile at Ida, and all but dropped my food in front of me with a disgusted curl on his lips.

"Is the spell still making you repel men?" Ida asked when the waiter had left. I blinked, uncomprehending, so she continued. "You told me you've been spelled."

I'd forgotten I'd done it. "I guess it's still on," I said lightly, but she leaned closer.

"So, who spelled you and how did that happen?"

I hadn't thought she'd be that interested. "Are you into the occult?"

She shrugged. "Something like that."

"Unfortunately, I have no answers to you. I was only joking."

She gave me a pointed look. "I didn't imagine that man's reaction, or how the men at the engagement party gave you a wide berth."

Curse her for being so observant.

But not for real. The last time I'd been able to curse people, it bounced back to me.

"Jack wasn't repelled by me," I said as calmly as I could. She tilted her head, considering me.

"That's true." Her eyes tightened minutely, the expression gone so fast I thought I'd imagined it. Then she picked up her fork and began to eat.

"So, what do you want to know about Jack?"

We had a great lunch talking about Jack and bashing men in general. I didn't learn anything useful, but it didn't hurt to have an ally in this wedding business, as she would be one of the bridesmaids. Her surprise about it rivalled mine.

"You'll meet my brother at the wedding too … provided you don't still repel men," she said with a laugh. She laughed a lot.

I ignored the jibe. "He wasn't at the engagement party?"

Saved by the Spell

"No, Julius is my stepbrother, a son of my mother's second husband and not related to the Sanford side of the family, but he'll be my date at the wedding—much to his horror."

I smiled. "Maybe he'll love it."

She laughed again, and this time there was a hard edge to it. "That'll be the day."

A shiver went down my bones for her tone. If I'd been more like my Aunt Clara, I would've interpreted it as an omen.

Since I wasn't, I returned to the office feeling pleased by the lunch.

I'd barely settled down behind my desk when Kane stormed in, badly startling me.

The startle turned into concern when I realised he wasn't wearing a jacket or waistcoat, and his shirtsleeves were rolled up. Had the magical strain of the previous day addled his brain?

He didn't *look* delirious. He was radiating with barely contained energy. "There you are! Come with me. I think I've found a solution."

Nine

"WHERE HAVE YOU BEEN THE WHOLE morning?" I asked as I followed him down the stairs and into the gallery. It was closed on Mondays, but the lights were on, which distracted me briefly.

Had they been on when I returned from lunch?

He led me to the exhibition space, and I paused at the door, my mouth hanging open.

"When did you do all this?"

The display cases holding the items waiting to be auctioned had been moved to the sides of the room to clear a large space in the middle. He had drawn a complicated diagram with chalk on the floor, with several candles placed on the proper spots.

My heart jumped. "You've found a way to break the spell?"

"Not yet," he said, with an apologetic look. "But I spent the morning at the council library and found a spell that will mask its effects on others."

"I guess that's better than nothing…"

It also explained why he hadn't answered his phone. One didn't keep the phone on in a library, even if no one else used said library.

"Infinitely better."

He picked up an old leatherbound notebook with scrawled handwriting and diagrams, the ink faded with age. "Now, let me see…"

He beckoned me to stand on a specific spot inside the diagram and then lit the candles with the wave of his hand. No matter how many times I saw him do that, it wouldn't stop impressing me.

Then he took a bunch of dried herbs and lit them with the candle placed on the northern compass point. It didn't start to burn with an open flame like I thought. Instead, it began to give out fragrant white smoke.

He started to sweep my body with the smoke, front and back.

"Are you cleansing my aura?" I asked, half jesting, but he nodded.

"Something like that. I'm opening it for the spell."

When he was done with the herbs—and a good thing too, because the scent made my nose itch and I was tolerably certain that violent sneezing would ruin the spell—he directed me to the western compass point and told me not move until he sat down. Then I was to do so too.

He stood opposite me on the pattern. He looked me straight in the eyes, the blue in them deeper than normal, as if they were glowing from the inside, and said one word in the mage language.

The pressure was sucked out of the room with a whomp, and my ears popped. He sat down, and I dropped to my knees less gracefully, my legs suddenly feeble.

Saved by the Spell

He began to chant, his voice strong and sonorous, the power behind every word making the candle flames dance and his hair billow more than usual. The air twirled around me, growing in power so that I felt like I was sitting in the eye of a tiny tornado. I couldn't pull my eyes away from him.

Abruptly, the wind died. I barely dared to breathe as Kane closed his eyes for a few heartbeats. He said one more word and it hit my solar plexus like a punch. Air whooshed out of me with a gasp.

The magic eased around us, and the candles died. Kane opened his eyes. His brows shot up and he blinked. Then he blinked again, and looked left and right, as if searching for something.

"Did it work?" I asked.

His eyes darted back to me. Shaking his head, he rubbed them with his thumb and middle finger, as if cleaning them. He opened them again, and sighed heavily. I didn't like the sound of it.

"Well, the good news is I'm not disgusted by your presence anymore."

Relief turned my bones liquid, and it took a moment before his words registered.

"There is bad news?"

His face was solemn like he was about to tell me I'd died. "The bad news is I can't see you anymore."

I stared at him, uncomprehending. "What do you mean?"

He grimaced. "It seems I've turned you invisible."

~ ~ ~

WE CLEANED THE GALLERY in silence. What was there to say after a turn like that?

I mopped the chalk lines off the floor and Kane moved the display cases back to their places. He avoided looking at me—or the mop that from his point of view was cleaning the floor by itself.

I didn't feel invisible. I could see myself normally, and I even appeared in a mirror. That was the first thing I checked.

"Maybe this is a gender specific spell too," I finally said as we climbed back upstairs. Kane went first so he wouldn't accidentally step on my heels. "Maybe women can see me fine."

"I don't know what it is. It shouldn't have had this effect in the first place."

"Can you undo it?"

"Yes," he stated firmly. "But not right now. I burned all the ingredients already. Let's get you home so that Amber and Giselle can help me."

He rolled down his sleeves and put on his waistcoat and jacket. I picked up my shoulder bag and he grimaced. "I'd best carry that."

I barely refrained from rolling my eyes, then remembered he couldn't see me and rolled them anyway as I handed him the bag.

The walk to his car took us through the plaza. The lunch rush was over and there weren't as many people around anymore, so I didn't accidentally bump into anyone. But I sighed in relief when I sat on the front seat of the Jag and Kane closed the door behind me.

He was normally that polite too, but this time it had the added benefit of not confusing the potential onlookers with the door opening and closing on its own.

"I'm really sorry about this," he said when we were on our way. "And I know it's not a consolation, but I truly

Saved by the Spell

feel better around you again. It was incredibly stressful before."

I still had no idea what to say to him. I wasn't angry as such; he'd tried his best and I didn't understand magic well enough to know what had gone wrong. But I couldn't just brush it aside either. This was a huge problem.

Although, I could see some benefits too…

"Maybe I could sneak into Jack's house while I'm invisible and look for the spell book he stole."

I was instantly excited about the idea. I could see myself sneaking silently through his home, with him none the wiser.

But Kane didn't share my enthusiasm. He turned to give me an admonishing look, only to startle when I wasn't there. He faced the traffic hastily again.

"That's still criminal activity. And incredibly dangerous."

I threw my hands up, the gesture wasted on him. "He stole it first," I said. "And what could be dangerous about it if he can't see me?"

"He might sense you there."

"He might not be home."

He spared me a glance. "Then you wouldn't have to be invisible in the first place."

I couldn't exactly argue with that logic.

"All I'm saying is, I am invisible, and it would be criminal to waste the opportunity it presents."

He was unmoved. "We'll reverse the spell immediately."

"Fine…"

I didn't want to frighten the customers of the magic shop, so we entered through the back door. But the place was empty, and Amber came to see who was there. Her brows shot up.

"Archibald? What brings you here in the middle of the day? Has something happened to Phoebe?"

So she couldn't see me either. Bugger.

"In a manner of speaking…" Kane said dryly, then gestured at where he assumed I was. I stepped forward, as if that helped.

"I'm here."

Amber was a former trauma nurse. She did not shake easily. But she staggered back now, turning pale. "What the hell happened?"

Kane looked contrite, probably for the first time ever. "I tried to mitigate the effects of Jack's spell, and it didn't work quite the way it should have."

"I'll say…" She pointed at the staircase. "Up you go, then. I'll close the shop."

Griselda was in the attic, lying in the middle of the floor, basking in a beam of sunlight filtering through the skylight. She opened her green eyes, annoyed for the interruption, and looked straight at me. She sprang up like being catapulted, her back arching like a bow and fur standing up, and hissed at me.

"I guess someone can sense me," I said, as the cat shot past me and out of the attic. I was a bit upset by her reaction. She'd often spent nights on my legs, and I'd grown accustomed having her there.

Kane stared after her, amazed. Then he looked at where he assumed I was standing. "We'll fix you."

I sighed. "What if you can't?"

"There's always someone who can," he assured me, reaching a hand as if to pat my shoulder, but dropping it as useless when he couldn't figure out where I was.

Saved by the Spell

"Do you have elders?" I asked, instantly curious. "Archmages or some such who are better at magic than all the rest?"

"We do, actually. Problem is, they're not easy to access."

"How so?"

He ran fingers through his hair. "They're old and tend to be cantankerous and reclusive. But they're powerful, to a point where I'm not entirely sure they are humans anymore."

"I thought none of the mages are humans."

He smiled, teasing, glancing at my general direction from the side of his eyes. "I thought we agreed that we're *enhanced* humans."

And I'd thought he hadn't caught my drift when I'd noted that he definitely was enhanced. Good thing he couldn't see me blush.

Giselle arrived, took in the scene—or what wasn't there, namely me—and shook her head. "Why did you have to try it on your own?"

"I happen to be a powerful mage," Kane said, defensively. "And it wasn't even a straining spell."

She didn't look mollified, and just held out a hand for the notebook Kane was carrying. She studied the contents for a few moments and then headed to her worktop to prepare the counter-spell.

"I was chosen to lead the mages on my skills, you know," he tried again, but she just glared at him and pointed at the shelf where the chalks were. He obeyed meekly enough.

The counter-spell took a long time to set, even with all three of them working on it, as it required constant consulting of the ancient notes, which were practically illegible. I eyed their proceeding with growing trepidation.

"What if this one turns me purple?"

"I've never heard of any spell doing that," Amber assured me.

"You'd never heard of a spell that makes a woman repulsive to men either."

She acknowledged it with a wry curl of her lips. "You don't really have a choice."

"I could wait and see if this goes away on its own."

They actually considered it briefly. But then Giselle shook her head. "I can't deal with an invisible lodger."

I inhaled, indignant. "But you can deal with a vampire and a werewolf?"

"They don't creep me out half as badly as you do, speaking out of nowhere."

In due course, I was told to take my place and they began. The counter-spell was remarkably similar to the original, and with the three of them casting it, the strength of it multiplied too. I was left gasping for breath after the last power word that activated it at the end.

They opened their eyes, and I could see from the way they relaxed and smiled—at me—that it had worked. Giselle pulled me into a hug.

"Thank the goddess. And you're not even purple."

Kane hugged me too, awkwardly. I smiled against his chest. "At least you're not repulsed by me anymore."

"Oh, I am," he said. "I just choose to ignore it for a moment."

Bugger.

Ten

KANE RELEASED ME AND RAN FINGERS through his thick hair, leaving it in disarray, a sign of his inner turmoil. "I think we should visit Rupert."

Amber nodded. "Great idea."

I studied them curiously. "Who's he?"

"The archmage," he explained, baffling me.

"I thought you said they are reclusive."

He smiled. "Yes, but if I don't give him time to hide, we might have a chance."

"Can I come too?" Giselle asked. "I'm overdue a visit."

Amber had to return to the shop, but the rest of us filed into Kane's Jag. The back seat wasn't exactly comfortable for my legs, but I tried not to complain. I couldn't sit at the front because Kane was repulsed by me again. Even the back seat was too close for his comfort, but he didn't complain.

Rush hour was starting, so the fifteen-minute drive north took about twenty-five minutes. Our destination was Highbury Fields in Islington, a fair-sized park with

Victorian villas and terraces on its western edge and modern blocks of flats on the east side.

Rupert Barnet, the archmage, lived in a Victorian villa on Highbury Crescent. It was a three-storey, two-family brown-brick with white trimmings, and columns in every architecturally possible place—and even a few spots that could have done without. The front garden was small, and his side of it was overgrown, the trees and bushes arching over the paved path to the front steps.

"He hasn't trimmed the garden the whole summer," Giselle muttered as she exited the car.

"He's over ninety, maybe even older than that," Kane reminded her. "He doesn't have the energy."

"He could ask for help. Or pay for it even."

They snorted a laugh.

I followed them through the wrought-iron gate and up the steps to a front door with paint flaking with age. Kane rang the doorbell, but if it worked I didn't hear it.

It took forever before I heard the lock being rattled on the other side, but Kane and Giselle waited patiently. The door was opened by an ancient man in a morning suit that had faded from black to greyish plum. His face consisted of wrinkles, and his white hair was so thin it was practically non-existent.

"Yes?" he asked in a faint voice, squinting at Kane, as if he couldn't see properly.

"Good afternoon, Jones. It's Archibald Kane and Mage Lynn to see the archmage."

"I'll inquire if Himself is receiving." He tottered around, and Kane followed him in.

"No need. We both know he'll deny the audience and I don't have time for that today."

Saved by the Spell

Giselle and I followed them into a gloomy hall. The tile floor was dusty, the drapes were drawn in front of the windows, and only one ancient lightbulb lit the place. But I could see that the hall had once been grand, and the antiques dealer in me was impressed by the furniture.

In a sedated pace, Jones led us down a hallway to a room at the back, gave the door a faint rap and opened it. "Mages Kane and Lynn and Miss…"

"Thorpe," Kane supplied.

"Miss Thorpe."

He received some sort of permission and stepped aside to let us into the room.

It was a parlour overlooking a lush garden, much larger than what I would have thought houses around here had. Afternoon sun was slanting through the leaves of the trees, illuminating the room with faint greenish light, the only light source it had. It revealed a room with faded Victorian wallpapers—probably red originally—and furniture that had likely been here since the house was built.

A man was seated in a tall wingback by the window, clad in a thick smoking jacket, with a red and green tartan blanket covering his legs. The room was chilly, but there was no fire in the fireplace. A large book sat on his lap.

For all that he could be a hundred, he didn't look nearly as old as Jones. His thick auburn hair had only a few, faint grey streaks, and his wrinkles were mostly around his eyes and on his forehead. He glared at us with sharp eyes.

"Kane. What's the meaning of this?"

Kane walked deeper into the room and bowed politely but remained standing. I stood by the door. Giselle had disappeared, likely with Jones.

"Rupert. I'm trying to locate a spell."

"There's a library at headquarters. Why don't you try there?"

"The book's been stolen from there."

The older man cackled. "Someone got through your wards?"

"Yes."

His admission added to Rupert's mirth, but he bore it well.

"Well, I don't see how I could help," Rupert said when he'd laughed enough.

"I was hoping to get a look at your library."

The amusement was instantly wiped away. "Absolutely not. You'll get the books once I'm gone and not a moment sooner."

Kane gave him a pointed look. "You've still not selected an apprentice?"

Rupert made a dismissive gesture. "There aren't decent mages around anymore to teach. What's wrong with the girl?"

The abrupt change of topic didn't faze Kane. "She's the reason I need your library. It's a medieval spell that protects unmarried women from unwanted male advances."

The archmage shot me a piercing look that made me quake in my boots. "You have an overprotective father, girl?"

I shook my head. "It was maliciously done by a mage."

"Who?"

"Jack Palmer," Kane answered for me.

The archmage snorted. "Hardly. He's not skilled enough."

"So you know the spell?"

Saved by the Spell

"I've heard of it. And it takes a great deal of power that he doesn't have."

Kane tilted his head in acknowledgement. "We think he had help casting it. And I've been unable to break it."

"Have you tried a kiss?"

Kane pulled back, and I felt stunned too. "A kiss?"

Jack had briefly kissed me the previous day, but that hadn't changed anything.

Our reaction amused the old man. "A true love's kiss no less. Medieval mages were always about clever tricks like that."

Kane nodded, regaining his composure. "A man who loves the woman so much that he's not deterred by the repulsion?"

"Could be." Rupert made a dismissive gesture with his hand. "Could be something else, like a blessing kiss of a father."

"Mine lives in France," I said, shoulders slumping. "And I don't have anyone who loves me so much they'd be able to resist the repulsion."

"Then you're in a pickle," Rupert said unhelpfully, but Kane was undeterred.

"But you never are, Rupert," he flattered shamelessly. "I know you could create the counter-spell even without studying the original."

"Save it, boy. Have you tried masking the effects?"

"Yes, but it turned her invisible."

Bushy auburn brows shot up. "Interesting side effect. Or maybe it worked as intended. You won't be repulsed by someone you can't see…"

He rolled his lips between his teeth as he pondered the problem. Then he nodded.

"Fine. I'll think of something. Come back tomorrow."

I would have wanted a faster solution, but I shouldn't expect miracles. Kane nodded.

"Thank you. Would six o'clock work?"

The door opened and Giselle wheeled in a tea tray. "I took inventory of your pantry. It's dismal. And I'll need to check your magic ingredients too."

"Leave it, you meddlesome woman. I don't cast spells anymore. I don't need ingredients."

She snorted. "You're the archmage. You'll stop casting spells the day you die."

"Just pour the tea…"

Kane took a seat on an armchair opposite Rupert, and Giselle and I sat on a sofa a little away. I was too wound up to drink, but I pretended to.

"So how come young Palmer targeted this human?" the archmage demanded to know.

"She's my assistant at the gallery," Kane explained. "Jack is helping someone to overtake the council, and this is their idea of a distraction. It's working too."

"Who?"

Kane took a sip of his tea. "I have no idea, but he's scary. He frightened even Danielle, and you know what she's like."

The bushy brows pressed down. "Blackhart."

"Who?"

"Julius Blackhart. He's from the north. Ellis's apprentice. Very nearly made it as his successor too, but Ellis changed his mind. Said there's something wrong with the fellow. Too close to becoming a warlock. But powerful."

Kane's eyes grew large in dismay. "And he wants to take over London?"

Saved by the Spell

"What else? If he can't make it into an archmage, and doesn't want to become a warlock, that's the greatest prize available."

Kane nodded. "That is useful information. Now we'll have to put a face to a name, so that we'll know who to keep an eye on for."

"Stay away from him," Rupert ordered. "Inconveniencing your assistant is small game for him."

I did not like the sound of that.

We finished the tea and the archmage promised to have the counter-spell by the next evening. "Bring the girl with you. We might as well take care of the matter here."

The mere notion of having that man perform a spell on me was frightening, but it was better than the alternative.

That the spell remained.

~ ~ ~

KANE DROPPED GISELLE AND me at the shop but didn't stay for dinner. We didn't need to ask why.

Setting the table while Giselle prepared the dinner, I asked her what I'd been wondering the whole drive home: "Why don't the archmages rule the mages?" Even I could tell that Rupert was powerful.

"They're not exactly reliable leaders. Their minds are too full of higher magic," she explained as she sautéed the pork loin. With a werewolf and a vampire living here, this was not a vegetarian household, although Giselle tried to introduce non-meat options every now and then too.

"They dedicate their lives to learning and improving spells. Moreover, they'd be too powerful for anyone to challenge for the leadership. If they happened to be a tyrant or otherwise inept to lead, we'd have no way of getting rid of them, especially since they live longer than regular mages. So they're excluded from the leadership."

"That sounds practical."

"It's bought with experience," she said dryly. "There's a spell over London enforcing it. Other places have something similar, but only large cities have truly powerful ones. It prevents archmages from rising to power and governs the leadership challenge in general. The words Archibald used after defeating Cynthia triggers it. It allows only one challenge per mage per cycle, and should the leader lose, transfers the power to the new leader."

I paused in the middle of the floor, squeezing a bouquet of forks and knives in my hand, as if repelling the realisation I had. "And now someone who's powerful enough to be an archmage but actually isn't wants to take over…"

She nodded, looking as queasy as I felt. "It must be the spell over London that lures him. Every mage donates a smidgen of their energy to it, keeping it constantly powered. In return, the council leader can use it to protect us. Imagine if someone close to being a warlock got their hands to it." She shook her head. "We can't let that happen."

"How will you stop him?"

"We'll have to band together. Defeat him before he can challenge Archibald, because if he has a chance to do that then we can't interfere. The spell makes sure of that too."

She took the frying pan off the stove and pointed at the cutlery I was holding, raising her brows in a not-so-subtle hint that I should do something about them. "With the magic of London to draw on, we might succeed."

Saved by the Spell

"Couldn't Rupert train one or more of you to counter this Blackhart?" I asked as I continued my task and she returned to hers.

"Archmages don't like to do that. They only train one, carefully selected successor at a time, so that the balance of power doesn't get distorted."

"And Rupert doesn't have a successor?"

She shook her head. "He wanted to train Danielle, but Kane talked him out of it."

"So she went to a warlock instead."

Warlocks started as mages, but they shed their humanity with human sacrifices. Kane's ex-wife was power hungry enough to try to learn from one. If she had become an archmage, she probably would've tried to take over the council too, prevention spell or not.

Giselle put the meat in the oven and closed the lid. "In hindsight, that's not much better, but at least she won't be our problem. But now Rupert has no successor."

"He didn't want to train Kane?"

She gave it a thought. "Possibly. Archibald has never had the same yearning for power as Danielle, so he may have refused. But if Rupert doesn't train someone soon, it might be too late."

"How many archmages are there? Couldn't one of them train a successor for Rupert?"

"No one knows their number for sure, but each of them has their own special spells and wards that they've perfected over the course of their long lives. If Rupert doesn't train someone, that knowledge will all be lost."

I could understand why it was vital he trained someone.

The next day, Giselle gave me a lift to work so that I wouldn't have to suffer the Tube—or be the cause of suffering there. It was bad enough that I distressed Kane with my mere presence, but at least he could close the door to his office. We passed the day by barely seeing each other.

However, he offered to drive me home after work so that we could go see Rupert together. He tried to hide how much it strained him, but a bead of sweat began to trickle down his temple long before we reached the House of Magic.

"Is the effect growing worse?" I asked, concerned.

"I think it is," he said, swallowing to ward off nausea. "But the good thing is, it'll be over tonight."

"What if Rupert hasn't found the counter-spell?"

He shot me an amused look. "He doesn't find spells. He creates them."

We had an early dinner before heading to Rupert's. Luca declared he would come with us too.

"Ashley said Kane needs a bodyguard." He was dressed for the role too, in black cargo trousers and a black T-shirt, his hair in a tight ponytail. The only thing missing was an earpiece and a mic on his collar.

Kane rolled his eyes, but he let Luca come. The two of them took Kane's Jag, much to Luca's pleasure. Giselle, Amber and I followed in Giselle's small Nissan.

Rupert's side of the house was dark. My gut tightened in disappointment as I imagined that Rupert had fled the house in order to keep us from intruding on his solitude. But then I remembered the drawn curtains and insufficient lights. He would be home.

Kane rang the doorbell. We waited for a long time, allowing Jones time to make his way slowly through the house, but nothing happened. He rang the bell again, and again we waited.

Saved by the Spell

Still nothing.

Frowning, he pushed the door and it opened. He didn't step in but checked the entrance for wards. The tightening of his face told me something was wrong before he spoke in a low voice: "These have been breached."

Luca's nostrils flared. "I smell blood."

Eleven

LUCA ENTERED THE HALL FIRST, stepping carefully like an agent in a movie. He didn't have to go far. Jones was standing in the middle of the hall, immobile with magic. He was barely conscious, his face pale and drawn. A trickle of blood was running down his nose and jaw, dropping on his once white shirt.

We rushed to him, stealth forgotten. Giselle reached to feel the pulse on his neck, and he opened his eyes, barely able to focus. Relief flushed through me, making my legs feeble.

"I can't smell anything beyond the blood," Luca said grimly. "Is anyone here?"

Jones was too exhausted to answer. Kane looked around with caution. "The spell would break if the caster was out of range."

Just then, the spell holding Jones up disappeared and he collapsed into Amber's and Giselle's arms. Luca and Kane rushed out the door in a desperate attempt to catch the attacker. Kane was fast, though not supernaturally fast like Luca, but if the assailant was in a car, they didn't stand a chance.

The women lowered Jones onto his back on the cold floor and elevated his legs. It didn't look like it helped, and his face retained its grey hue.

Luca and Kane returned a moment later, looking furious. "If the attackers were nearby when we arrived, they're gone now."

Jones opened his eyes. "Black ... hart."

We looked each other, stunned.

Kane kneeled by him. "Did he attack you?"

"Took ... Himself. Couldn't ... stop." A tear fell down his wrinkly cheek. He lost consciousness again.

"We need to get him to a hospital," Amber declared.

Luca crouched and gathered the frail old man into his arms as if he didn't weigh anything. He carried Jones out of the door and into Giselle's car, with the women following. I watched them go, anxious and helpless.

"What should we do now?" I asked Kane. He was standing in the middle of the hall, hands squeezed into tight fists and hair billowing with barely contained fury.

He unclenched his jaw with effort. "We find Rupert. And then we find this Blackhart and make him pay."

I was fine with that plan.

Luca returned, and together we went through the ground floor, a slow job because Kane had to check every door for magical boobytraps. There were none, and no one was lurking there to attack us.

The next floor was gloomy and quiet, and empty too. The last room towards the back garden was a large study. A desk lamp was on, illuminating a messy desk. The chair was overturned, and papers and books were lying on the floor.

"It looks like there was a struggle," Luca noted. He took a whiff. "I smell at least two people, maybe three."

Saved by the Spell

Kane's jaw tightened. "It can't have been much of a struggle. Rupert is powerful but he's old. If this Blackhart is as powerful as Rupert claims, he could've easily overpowered him if he took Rupert by surprise."

"But why?"

I studied the messy room, perplexed. Tall hardwood shelves lined the walls, but they were curiously empty. Had Blackhart wanted Rupert's books and taken him too?

Then a thought hit me, and my stomach tightened painfully. "Was it our fault?"

Had Blackhart taken Rupert so that he couldn't help us?

"I don't think so," Kane consoled me. "Maybe Blackhart came to demand that Rupert make him an archmage, maybe he wanted Rupert to back him in taking over the council."

I tried to believe him. The alternative was too horrible.

"Do you think he's still alive?"

Kane stood in the middle of the floor, hands on his hips as he studied the room. He gestured to the shelves. "Yes. The wards hiding his library are still up. They'll come down the moment he dies."

So that's why the shelves looked empty.

"How do we find him?"

He glanced at me from under his brows. "We'll trace him."

He went to wide double doors to the adjoining room and opened them to reveal a large, empty space. Old traces of chalk on the parquet floor revealed that this was where Rupert cast his spells. The shelves there were empty too, but the spell ingredients were probably hidden like the books.

Or Giselle was right, and he had used up everything.

"We need a personal item of his," Kane said, conjuring a piece of chalk from somewhere. "Something he would've touched often."

"His reading glasses?" I suggested, and Luca and I went to look. They weren't on his desk, so they'd likely gone with him—or were hidden underneath the clutter on the floor. We stared at the messy desk for inspiration.

"How about that fountain pen?" I asked, pointing at the ancient looking thing. I couldn't believe it would still be in use, but it lay on the desk as if he'd been recently writing with it.

"Let's give it a try."

Luca pulled out a hem of his shirt and picked up the pen with it so as not to leave his essence on it. I followed him back to the casting room, where Kane had drawn a surprisingly small pattern on the floor, only large enough for a small portable item. He told Luca to set the pen in the middle of it.

"Don't you need a map?" I asked, remembering the previous tracing spell they'd done.

"No, I'll spell the pen so that it'll lead to Rupert."

Luca and I retreated to the side of the room to watch him cast the spell. He wrapped an arm around my waist, the gesture consoling.

"Don't you find me repulsive anymore?" I wanted to press my head on his shoulder, but I didn't want to make him throw up.

"I do, but you needed a hug, so I'm enduring."

Tears blurred my eyes, and it took a long time before I could see clearly.

The spell was rather disappointing to watch, and fast to cast. Kane picked the pen up. Then he frowned. "I can

Saved by the Spell

feel that the spell has taken, but it's not pulling me anywhere."

"What does that mean?"

Luca leaned closer. "Is he still in the house?"

Kane shook his head, disappointed. "No. I'm afraid Rupert is already out of range."

~ ~ ~

"What now?"

I had no idea what to do, and no suggestions to make. I was an excellent antiques dealer's assistant, capable of handling even the trickiest situations involving anything from items that turned out to be stolen to out and out forgeries, but I hadn't had to deal with abductions before.

Kane was squeezing the pen like he wanted to throw it against the wall, but in the end he just slipped it into the breast pocket of his jacket and got up.

"First, we'll go through Rupert's desk, in case he made notes of the spell that'll break yours."

I'd completely forgotten why we'd come here. The realisation that I still wouldn't be rid of the spell threatened to bring tears back to my eyes, and I had to blink to keep them down. With Jones in the hospital and Rupert missing, the spell was a minor problem.

Luca patted me on the shoulder and guided me after Kane to study the desk.

There were dozens, if not hundreds of notes on loose sheets of paper scattered on the floor after the struggle with Blackhart. We collected every paper we could find, and Kane went through them carefully. But in the end, he had to give up.

"If one of these does the trick, I seem to be unable to figure it out."

He looked so angry with himself that I rested my hand on his arm—briefly, so that I wouldn't make him feel worse.

"We'll find Rupert and he'll break the spell," I said with more optimism than I felt.

"But how?" Luca asked. "Magic's failed us, and I can't track them beyond the street where they got into a car."

I rubbed my face vigorously to get the blood flowing to my brain. "How about instead of trying to find Rupert, we try to find Blackhart?"

Kane shook his head. "What do you think I've been trying to do this past month? If the council members know who he is or where to find him, they're too afraid to talk."

"Jack knows who he is."

"We presume. We have no idea if it's Blackhart he's helping."

I wanted to growl in frustration, but I wasn't ready to give in. The only person who could help me was being held captive by an evil mage, and I needed him found—for me as well as for his own safety.

So how about finding someone even more evil…

A smile spread on my face, and I had a notion it was a smidgen evil too. "We'll ask someone who isn't afraid of him."

Kane gave me a puzzled look. "Who?"

"Danielle."

He practically jumped back in his haste to reject my suggestion. "No!"

"Oh come on. She's the only one who can help."

"There's no saying what she can or cannot do." He crossed arms over his chest, rejecting my suggestion with

Saved by the Spell

his entire body. "But the point is moot. I don't know how to reach her."

The last we'd seen her she'd stepped through a portal and vanished with her warlock partner.

"Surely someone must know how to reach her. Her parents?"

Kane just shook his head.

"I can try to track her down," Luca suggested. "I've occasionally done cyber searches."

"Excellent," I said before Kane could torpedo that idea too. "Let's go home."

After renewing the wards on Rupert's door, Kane drove us home. And even though he didn't look at all willing, he followed us in and down to the basement, where Luca had his lair.

Though that wasn't exactly an accurate word.

His room was twice the size of mine, taking the entire width of the basement, with an en suite bathroom and a walk-in closet. The colour scheme was the same grey and white as the rooms upstairs, and nothing indicated that the room belonged to a century-old vampire.

It looked like it belonged to a single man under thirty: messy and full of gadgets.

There was a large desk on one wall with several computer monitors side by side, most of them on and showing stock market data. Luca supported himself with trading and online poker, the two sides of the same coin, as he'd told me one night when I kept him company during a poker tournament.

He was excellent at both, and he could have lived on his own somewhere more luxurious, but he preferred having friends around. Especially the kind that knew what he was.

He took a seat at the desk and clicked the keyboard, bringing one more monitor to life. "Now, let me see…"

He began the search, with Kane and I watching over his shoulder—though Kane's attention seemed to be on the stock markets.

"Here," Luca said after a suspiciously short search.

"You'd tracked her down already, hadn't you," I said, and he shot me an impish grin.

"She's both hot and dangerous. I thought it prudent to keep an eye on her." He got up and gestured at the chair. "Will you do the honours?" he said to Kane, who looked like he'd rather be anywhere else.

Like at the dentist having his teeth pulled out.

But he sat on the vacated chair and placed his hand on the mouse. "It's late in France," he said.

"It's only a little past eight there."

Luca had everything ready for a Skype call. He'd even used Kane's email address—and how he knew that I had no idea—so that Danielle would know the call came from him. All Kane had to do was click the icon that connected the call.

He stretched his neck and drew a fortifying breath. I tried to sympathise—their divorce had been ugly—but the longer he dawdled, the farther Blackhart could move Rupert.

"Shall I do it for you?"

My tone was more sarcastic than I intended, but it had the desired effect. He placed the call.

We waited tensely for Danielle to answer. It seemed to take forever, but happened so fast that she managed to surprise us when her face appeared on the monitor, puzzled and disdainful.

"Archie?"

Saved by the Spell

She was a beautiful woman a couple of years older than Kane, dainty with a sharp chin, slightly downturned green eyes, full lips, and asymmetrically cut rich brown hair that fell partly over her face. There were faint lines in the corners of her eyes and mouth, and she radiated strength and power even through a video connection.

Kane cleared his throat. "Hello, Danielle. I trust you're well?"

I punched him in the shoulder. This was not a social call.

Danielle noticed it and she sneered. "I can see you've your *assistant* with you." She thought we were dating and wouldn't accept the truth. "And a pet vampire too."

"Hey! I'm not his pet," Luca said indignantly. "I'm Phoebe's."

I shot him a grin. Anything to aggravate Danielle.

Though we should keep it to minimum. We did need her help.

"What do you want?" she asked impatiently. "I'm in the middle of a dinner."

"I need you to tell me everything you know about Blackhart," Kane said.

A smirk twisted her lips. "So you found out about him, did you?"

"No thanks to you," I interjected, but she ignored me.

"Why would I tell you anything?"

Her tone irritated me, but Kane was in better control of his emotions, and he studied her calmly. "Blackhart has taken Rupert and we need to find him before he does something drastic."

Her brows shot up. "So he's moving on with the plan…"

"What plan?" Kane demanded.

Before she could answer, a man appeared next to her. He looked to be in his early forties, with a starkly handsome face, a very French aquiline nose, and a hint of grey at the temples of his black hair.

Laurent Dufort, the warlock Danielle had hooked up with in order to learn dark magic, and an overall sexy guy—for someone evil and probably a hundred and fifty years old.

He kissed her on the cheek. "The dinner is growing cold, *cherié.*"

A warm smile softened her face. If we'd had any doubt the two were an item, that banished it. "I'll be right there."

Dufort directed his black eyes at us, and even through the video link I could feel their impact. I almost took a step back, halting myself only by grabbing the back of Kane's chair.

"Why are you contacting Danielle?" His French pronunciation made the name sound like a caress, even though his tone was sharp.

Kane wasn't intimidated by him. "Her former accomplice has kidnapped the archmage of London and we need any information she has to locate them."

He cocked a gently admonishing brow at her. "Is this true, *cherié?*"

"How should I know?" She glared at us. "What do you think I can do? I don't live in London anymore."

"Just tell us who he is, where he lives, and who his companions are," I said.

"Oh, is that all."

Kane's jaw tightened at her mocking tone. "Need I remind you that Rupert is old and might die?"

"If he'd chosen his successor, that wouldn't matter."

As if that was all we cared about!

Saved by the Spell

"And if you weren't such a power-hungry bitch, he might have chosen you," I spat.

Her eyes flashed in anger, and Dufort placed a hand on her shoulder. "She'll have the information to you by morning."

He cut the connection.

"That went well," Luca said dryly.

I was still seething with anger. "The nerve of that woman. Doesn't she have any compassion?"

Kane's mouth curled in a bitter twist. "Not really."

"Now what do we do? We have nothing to go on."

Kane ran a hand through his hair and got up. "I guess we'll find Jack and ask him about Blackhart, in case he's involved after all."

Luca took a seat and began to search for the address, but he had to shake his head. "There are hundreds of that name, and I can't even be sure he's one of them."

Kane patted him on the shoulder. "No matter. Council headquarters should have his address." He glanced at his watch. "It's still early. Let's go."

Twelve

THE LONG DRIVE TO THAMES DITTON passed in silence. Even Luca was deep in his thoughts, which wasn't a natural state for him.

"What if Jack isn't in league with Blackhart?" I had to ask. I hated that I sounded hopeful still. Kane's mouth tightened.

"That would be a point in his favour, but it won't help Rupert."

"How's the pen?"

"Growing cold."

I leaned closer in alarm, and he leaned away, unconsciously. It was as if I had a force-field he reacted to. "What does that mean?"

"That he's either being moved farther away, or we're moving away from him."

Since we were driving away from central London, I hoped it was the latter.

The parking lot of the retirement home had quieted for the night, but there were a couple of cars. Remembering Cynthia's attack on Sunday, I looked around carefully when I exited the car, but there was no one around.

The headquarters was dark too, but the mages had some sort of permanent spell or ward in place to make it appear like it was empty. Luca insisted on going in first, and Kane let him, shaking his head, exasperated.

I thought his attitude was much too cavalier, after what had happened to Rupert and Jones, but kept my mouth shut for once.

Lights were on in the hall, but no one was around, and Luca couldn't hear anything either. Kane checked his wards on the library door.

"These are intact." He peeked into the library, but it was dark.

"Someone must be here," I said, but Luca grinned.

"Or mages are careless with lights."

Kane acknowledged his assessment with a wry tilt of his head, but pointed deeper into the building. "I think we'd best search the place anyway."

"I'll take point," Luca stated, but Kane disagreed.

"If there is a mage here, he's either on an innocent errand or here to challenge me, in which case they should be allowed to."

"That doesn't mean you have to let them take you by surprise," Luca countered, and went in first.

We started from the upper floor, where the offices and a large open space for casting spells were. The place was dark and empty, and according to Luca's nose, no one had been there that day. No one was on the ground floor either.

"Let's head to the cellar."

We followed Kane to an erstwhile vestry of the priory the place had once been. Spiral stone steps led down to a

Saved by the Spell

vaulted cellar where the mages kept their wine, safe, and a club to hang out in after strenuous spellcasting.

Lights were on in there, and we slowed, treading as quietly as we could, but the stone vaults echoed anyway. Large columns obscured our view to the club at the far end. We crept past them towards the light source—and paused in surprise.

Jack was standing behind the bar, pouring himself a drink. He looked up when he spotted us and made a sweeping gesture towards the shelf of bottles behind him.

"May I offer you a drink before we begin?"

I stared at him in dismay. Even knowing he'd put the spell on me, I hadn't wanted to find him at the centre of things. "What are you doing here?"

Luca took a protective stance in front of me. "Who is he?"

"Jack Palmer," Kane provided, regarding Jack calmly.

"The bastard who put the spell on you?" A growl made Luca's body vibrate, and I placed a calming hand on his shoulder, though I wasn't entirely composed myself and the hand shook a little.

Jack smirked at Luca. "You don't seem to be affected by it."

"Vampires are special," he countered, but his muscles were tense under my hand, and I let it drop.

We walked to the bar, but kept our distance of Jack. He gave me a slow once-over, his turquoise eyes gleaming. It would've made me feel wanted before, but now it only aggravated me, banishing my nervousness.

"So … are you ready for the spell to come off?" he drawled.

My heart sped up, but I wasn't that naïve. "In exchange for what?"

He faced Kane. "You concede the council for me ... and I'll break the spell."

Kane's eyes sharpened, and he looked like he was genuinely considering his suggestion. I kicked him in the ankle—lightly; he was my boss—startling him. I glared at Jack.

"He will not."

"It's not really your choice, is it," Jack said to me, but Kane had come to his senses.

"She's the one affected by the spell, so it is her choice."

Jack leaned his hands on the bar. "And you're unable to break it without me. So how about it?"

"That's not an acceptable challenge for my position," Kane countered, "so how about you tell us everything you know about Blackhart, and I'll let you challenge me the proper way."

Jack paled. "I don't know who you're talking about."

"Right..." Kane's tone was dry. "You did not break the wards on the library door by yourself."

Jack looked like he'd deny taking part in it too, but thought the better of it. "It wasn't Blackhart."

"Who, then?"

"No one you know."

Kane's brows shot up. "I know all the mages in London."

"Are you sure?" Jack taunted him. Since Blackhart had been operating in London for months already, with Kane none the wiser, he didn't answer.

"Where can I find Blackhart?"

"You don't want to find him."

"No, but I want to find Rupert, and Blackhart has him," Kane stated. Jack pulled back.

Saved by the Spell

"How do you know about that?"

So he wasn't even trying to deny his involvement. Disappointment brought bile to my mouth.

"We arrived at Rupert's only moments after you took him. We had to take Jones to hospital after what you did to him."

"I had nothing to do with that," Jack denied vehemently, but I sneered, not believing him.

"That's not plausible deniability."

His eyes flashed, and a light flush rose to his cheeks. "I was the driver."

"Right…"

"Just tell us where Rupert is," Kane said sternly, "and I won't kick you out of the council for this."

His threat had no effect on Jack. "I'll tell you if you concede the council to me."

I looked at him with contempt. "Are you so weak you can't even challenge him to a proper duel?"

He huffed. "Hardly."

And he attacked Kane.

I jumped behind Luca's back with a small shriek, the flash of Jack's spell blinding me briefly. But Kane had been expecting the move. He had his defences ready—and an attack spell too.

And this time, he wasn't being gentlemanly.

Jack had barely parried the first attack when Kane was already slinging the next spell. Even with the bar between them, the energy ball hit Jack, stunning him. He collapsed on the floor and stayed there, unable to move.

That was embarrassingly fast.

Luca and I reached to look over the bar to see if Jack would rally again, but he was only able to glower at us. Kane rounded the bar and stood above Jack, staring down at him with more calm than I would've thought he possessed in this situation.

"In front of these witnesses, you challenged me for the leadership of the council of mages, yes?" he asked, the same question he'd asked Cynthia, evoking the spell protecting London.

But Jack wasn't as ready to accept his defeat as she had been. He glared furiously at Kane, who repeated the question until Jack spat an angry, "Yes."

"In front of these witnesses, your challenge was accepted, yes?"

Jack nodded, the gesture minute.

"You'll have to state it aloud, otherwise the spell won't recognise it," Kane said.

"Yes," Jack growled.

"And in front of these witnesses, I won and you lost, yes?"

"Yes."

"As I free you, you agree not to challenge me again during this leadership cycle?"

If looks could kill, Jack's surely would have. It took him a physical effort to get the words out. "I agree."

Kane offered him a hand, and freed from the spell, Jack accepted it—with ill grace. Luca and I watched them tensely, both of us certain that Jack would attack again the moment he was up, but he didn't.

Kane nodded at us. "The magical formula is binding," he explained. "He's physically unable to attack me, or my successor should I lose, until the next time the leadership is open for a challenge."

Tension in my shoulders released and I leaned heavily against the bar.

Saved by the Spell

"You may think you've won, but this isn't over," Jack spat.

"Why don't you get off your huff and behave like a grownup," Kane drawled, the tone not very conducive to creating good will between them.

But Jack ignored him and shot me a sneer. "You should've accepted my offer. If you think your spell is bad, wait until you see what I have in store for your cousin."

Before I could find my tongue to answer, he crossed the cellar and disappeared up the stairs.

"That didn't go the way I expected," Luca said, breaking the silence that had followed Jack out. Kane shook his head, looking grim.

"If that battle was the best he had to offer, I have no idea how he was able to break my wards, or cast that spell on you."

"Blackhart must be helping him more than we thought."

But he didn't look convinced. "What I've learned of him so far, he doesn't seem like a helpful person."

He was right. "So is there a third person in play, one we don't know anything about?"

"He's recruited our mages to his schemes before, and I've already dealt with most of them—or Blackhart has."

"So an unknown…"

That wasn't good.

"I don't like that he's threatening your cousin," Kane said, but I wasn't worried.

"She can handle herself. I'm more worried about Rupert. How do we find him now?"

His lip curled into smile. "I placed a tracking spell on Jack when I helped him up. Where he goes, we can follow."

"What are we waiting for, then? He could lead us to Rupert. Let's go."

Energised once more, we hurried up and through the building to the front door. There Kane insisted going to the car first, in case Jack had left traps on it.

Turned out, there were no traps. He'd done worse.

He'd blown out all the tyres with magic.

~ ~ ~

IT WAS LATE WHEN LUCA and I exited a taxi outside the magic shop. Kane had left the car where it was to deal with it later, and we'd dropped him off at his house on our way.

He hadn't spoken much, and he hadn't suggested we take his other car and search for Jack.

The way his hair had been billowing with anger and his mouth set in a tight line, Luca and I hadn't dared to suggest it either.

Giselle and Amber were in the kitchen, drinking tea. They looked tired, but they straightened expectantly when we entered.

"Where have you been?" Amber asked. "We've been worried."

"We were trying to locate Rupert," I said, slumping in a chair. "How's Jones?" I didn't even know his first name.

"They're keeping him overnight," Giselle said, getting up to take out more cups. "But there shouldn't be anything seriously wrong with him."

Saved by the Spell

"But he's old, so…" Amber added, and I grimaced. Anything could happen after an ordeal like he'd been through. "I take it you didn't find Rupert?"

"Not for lack of trying," Luca said dryly. "Blackhart is really good at making people keep their mouth shut. We didn't even get Danielle to talk."

That Kane had contacted her understandably amazed the women. We told them everything that had happened that evening.

"That was petty of Jack," Giselle noted when we finished with the description of the poor Jag with its tyres reduced to pieces.

"Kane took it surprisingly well," Luca said, shaking his head. "I would've gone on a rampage."

So would I, but for a man with a temper, he'd kept his fury reined in.

"I wouldn't have thought Jack was a poor loser," I said, ashamed that I'd been so taken with his beautiful eyes. "And he wasn't nearly as skilled as we'd imagined."

"Who do you think it was who helped him to break the library wards?" Giselle asked Amber, but her wife shook her head.

"If they're not from London, it's impossible to tell."

"Has there been any strange mages visiting the shop?" I asked. "They must get the ingredients for their spells somewhere."

Amber shook her head, but Luca disagreed. "I don't know all the mages personally, so it's entirely possible that they've been here, maybe keeping an eye on us."

I shuddered. Amber pursed her mouth into a line.

"We'll learn it eventually. I'm more worried about Jack threatening Phoebe's cousin."

To my shame, I'd completely forgotten about it. "What do you think he'll do?"

I hoped it wasn't the same spell he'd cast on me. That would make for an awkward wedding if the groom was repulsed by the bride.

I didn't sleep well that night. And by "not well" I mean at all, the events of the evening twirling in my mind. I was seriously considering calling in sick in the morning—Kane wouldn't mind, since I literally made him sick—but I managed to drag myself to the kitchen at the usual hour, relatively put-together.

Ashley was having breakfast, looking fresher after her twenty-four-hour shift than I did. She shot me a puzzled look. "You look like shit."

"Thanks."

Since Giselle wasn't there cooking and I had no energy for it, I poured myself a large mug of coffee and sat next to her. I told her what had happened last night, and she grew angrier as the story progressed.

"I'll drive you to work. In case the little shit tries to retaliate."

"I don't want to trouble you after your long shift," I hedged, though the offer was tempting.

But she snorted. "It was nothing. We didn't even have any alarms. I've practically slept the whole night."

Since it was more sleep than I'd had, I accepted her offer. I didn't fear that Jack would attack me, but I didn't feel like tackling the commute.

Morning traffic was horrible, but I wasn't in a hurry. Kane could manage his tea himself this once. I had a comfortable seat in Ashley's Range Rover, and I didn't have to drive.

Saved by the Spell

Despite the best efforts of the Central London traffic, we reached the antique shop eventually. Since Ashley couldn't drive into the pedestrian court, she parked the car—illegally—by the street and walked me the rest of the way.

"Is this really necessary?" I protested, but she stared at me down her nose, eerily like her wolf had done the other day, and I gave in.

"In that case, would you like the world's greatest blueberry muffin?"

Her face lit up. "Absolutely."

I led her to my favourite café, happy to have her with me as a buffer. The usual morning crowd filled the place, everyone so sleepy that they didn't even react when a six-foot-one bald amazon walked in. I bet that didn't happen to her often.

Jack wasn't there. But as I was queueing, the sensation that someone was watching me suddenly returned, burning my neck as if it had a physical presence.

I resisted rubbing the spot. If Jack wasn't here, who or what was causing the sensation?

Surreptitiously, I moved to stand right in front of Ashley so that she blocked my back, but the sensation remained. Was I imagining it?

I studied every reflective surface to look behind me, but the woman in line behind Ashley had her eyes glued to her phone and I couldn't see her face. No one else was looking at me either. With Ashley there, no one would.

We got our orders and I hurried out of the café, not looking left or right, but the sensation followed me. I rushed across the court to the gallery, with puzzled Ashley at my heels.

"Are you late for work?"

"No, but I feel like someone's watching me."

She turned to study the court as I opened the door to the offices and switched off the alarm.

"I don't see anyone watching you."

I shuddered. "I must be imagining it, but I've felt it for days now. Usually on the Tube."

"Maybe someone's keeping an eye on you with magic, over a distance."

My knees buckled, and she reached to steady me. "They can do that?"

"Shit, I don't know. It's just a thought."

"I'll ask Kane."

She walked me all the way to my desk and then went through the rooms to see that no one was lurking there.

"Thanks for the ride," I said when she was convinced the office was safe.

"Thanks for the muffin," she countered, lifting the bag. "And if you need a ride home, just call me. I'm free until morning."

I said I would, but I had no intention of troubling her more today.

I was running late, so I hurried to make Kane's tea. I had everything ready when I heard the door open downstairs. I put on my professional smile—though he had an unnerving skill of seeing through it—and faced the door.

Olivia walked in.

"Oh my God, I'm so glad you're here," she said—and burst into tears.

Thirteen

I HURRIED TO MEET HER AND SHE collapsed on me, sobbing in delicate gulps. She was smaller than me, but her full weight was on me, almost making me collapse.

I glanced around, as if help would miraculously materialise, but apparently magic didn't work that way, because I was alone.

Out of options, I walked Olivia to Kane's office and the sofa there. He wouldn't like that I invaded his private space, but it couldn't be helped.

"What's happened?" I asked once I had her settled and equipped with a tissue.

"Henry ... broke off the engagement," she hiccupped.

My entire body went cold, and I had to sit down too.

"Just like that?"

Was this Jack's doing?

It couldn't be. Maybe Olivia and Henry had had an epic fight; maybe they'd realised they'd become engaged too hastily. Perfectly normal explanations.

She wiped her eyes with the tissue, careful not to smudge her makeup. "He woke up this morning and asked who I was. And not like it was a joke. He genuinely had no idea. He was scared and then he got angry, and he threw me out."

Well then … not normal. And far worse than I could have imagined.

But I still searched for an explanation other than Jack's meddling. "Had he been in an accident? Hit his head maybe?"

"No. Everything was fine last night, and then—bam." She paused to blow her nose. Daintily.

"I tried to tell him we're engaged and about to get married, but he refused to even hear me. And then he spotted the engagement ring and demanded I give it back, because it belonged to his grandmother."

She buried her face in her hands and started to sob again. I patted her back, at a loss for words. Kane appeared at the door just then, took in the scene, and froze. The look of utter horror on his face would have been comical in any other situation.

Sorry, I mouthed at him, and he beat a hasty retreat, closing the door behind him.

"What are you going to do now?" I asked my cousin.

"I don't know. I love him so much and it destroys me that he doesn't even remember me."

"Could he be pretending for some reason?"

She lifted her head and shot me an offended look. "What reason could there possibly be?"

I gestured with my free hand. "I don't know. Guys get cold feet all the time, and you were moving so fast. Maybe he took a more brutal approach."

She wiped her eyes with the backs of her hands, spreading the mascara. "What could possibly have changed during the night?"

Saved by the Spell

I knew the answer to that, but I couldn't reveal it to her. "Night is the time when all the nasty worries take over."

"Henry isn't like that. He would've told me about his worries."

Since I didn't know him, I nodded. But with only a couple of months acquaintance, how well did she know him either?

"Have you tried calling him since?"

"Yes, but he won't answer my calls. Could you do something?"

I dropped my hand as if she'd burned me. "Me? I don't even know him."

"But you got along so well with Jack," she pleaded, placing a hand on my arm. Even red-rimmed and smudged like raccoon's, her dove-eyes were effective. "Maybe you could talk to him together."

Hell would freeze over before that happened. "Maybe you should call Jack yourself and ask him to help." He wouldn't, but at least I wouldn't have to get involved.

Only, I already was.

Bugger.

I patted the hand on my arm. "Fine. I'll see what I can do. But I'm not promising results. Maybe Henry has a medical condition that caused a sudden amnesia. And if he's faking it, he really must not want to marry you to pull off something this stupid."

She straightened and drew a fortifying breath. "If he truly doesn't want to marry me, I'll understand. But I want to know why."

"That's perfectly understandable."

Pity I couldn't tell her the truth.

With my promise, Olivia recovered from her bout of crying. She headed to the loo to wash her face and redo her makeup, and I wandered into my side of the office space. Kane was sitting at my desk, working at his laptop.

He shot me a glare. "I hope this sort of drama won't become a habit."

"Absolutely not," I hastened to assure him. Then I reconsidered. "Well, it depends on Jack."

His brows shot up, but Olivia emerged from the loo just then, looking her usual ethereal self, and Kane rose hastily, his face softening. He wasn't immune to her power either.

She smiled and apologised prettily for the intrusion, and he was perfectly willing to forgive her, bowing a little for further measure.

The twinge inside me wasn't jealousy. It was envy. He never treated me with that much tolerance.

I saw Olivia downstairs and to the door. Kane was standing by his office when I returned up. "To my office, please."

"I really am sorry about that," I said as I followed him to his desk. "I'd say it's not my fault, but it kind of is."

Or his.

He took a seat behind his desk, gesturing me to do the same. "Let's hear it, then."

I slumped on the guest chair. "Henry broke off the engagement with my cousin Olivia. That was her right now." I told him everything Olivia had told me. "It was Jack's revenge, like he threatened yesterday. He's somehow made him fall out of love with her."

He considered my explanation with a deep frown. "There isn't a spell that can make two people fall in love—

Saved by the Spell

or out of it. Mages have tried over the millennia, but no one's managed it."

"Well, Jack must have managed it, or Blackhart. What else could explain it?"

"Based on what you told me, he must have used a spell that made Henry forget your cousin. That one does exist."

I stared at him stunned. Then my blood surged in fury. "That rat bastard! What an awful thing to do."

"It is," he admitted, looking angry too. "And he couldn't have done it alone."

"Blackhart." I almost spat the name.

He nodded. "Or the mystery mage who helped him earlier, if we presume Blackhart isn't exactly a helpful person."

"Can we undo it?"

"We can certainly try," he assured me, and I smiled, relieved that he was willing to help.

"Meanwhile, I could try to find out if Henry is just acting."

He shot me a worried look. "You're not going to talk to Jack, are you?"

I shuddered. "Absolutely not. I couldn't promise not to punch him."

Although that would be satisfying…

"I'll talk to Ida, Henry's cousin."

"What good will that do?"

He was genuinely puzzled, and I couldn't blame him. "If he's faking it, she could talk sense into him." Another thought occurred. "And she seems to know Jack well too. Maybe she could talk to him."

"And tell him what?" He gave me a pointed look. "That he shouldn't use magic against ordinary humans?"

I made a face. "No. Although, she did take it well when I told her I was spelled to repel men."

He pulled back. "Why would you tell her that?"

"She noticed how men were behaving around me, and it sort of came out," I said, a tad defensively. I was perfectly aware that I shouldn't have done it. "But I don't think she actually believed me."

"Well, I guess it wouldn't hurt to talk to her. At the very least, you could get Jack's address from her."

After everything, we'd forgot to look it up the previous night.

I sent Ida a message, but before she had a chance to answer, Kane's phone rang. His grimace told me clearly who it was.

Danielle.

He put it on video call. "Have you anything for me?" He didn't waste time for pleasantries this time, although he looked like the omission pained him. That, or speaking with Danielle did.

"I have Blackhart's address, but I doubt he's keeping Rupert there."

My body quickened in expectation. Now we were in business.

Kane nodded. "If nothing else, it gives us a chance to keep an eye on him."

"I'd stay clear of him," she warned. "You don't know what he's capable of."

"Do you know who his associates are?" Kane asked.

"Apart from Palmer? Random people in the community. But he brought someone with him when he came to London. A relative. I've never met her, so I don't know how powerful a mage she is, but she's the only one who has any sway over him."

Saved by the Spell

Perhaps we should try with her.

"What's her name and where can we find her?"

"I have no idea."

That was helpful.

Kane thanked Danielle, and finished the call. A moment later his phone pinged for an incoming message.

"We have the address. Let's go and see where that leads us."

~ ~ ~

KANE POPPED INTO THE GALLERY to tell Mrs Walsh that we'd be gone for the day. I waited for him outside, taking the chance to study the window display with a critical eye. I saw it every day and had stopped paying attention to it. But Mrs Walsh never failed, and it looked excellent as always.

While my back was turned to the court, the pressure in my neck suddenly returned.

I swirled around, determined to finally find the source, but people were passing through the court in droves, it seemed, and I couldn't detect anyone.

Kane exited the gallery and gave me a puzzled look. "Is something amiss?"

"The pressure in my neck is back. Ashley said it could be someone keeping an eye on me from a distance with magic. Is that possible?"

He glanced around too. "I guess it could be," he said dubiously. "Some version of the location spell I put on Jack. Do you think he put one on you?"

Since that was exactly what I'd thought, I nodded. "But he's not here, is he?"

"No. The spell would tell me."

"So where is it coming from?"

Just then, someone hailed me from the door of my favourite café, and the tension in my neck disappeared. Ida.

"That's Henry's cousin," I said to Kane, heading across the court. "I have to talk with her."

"Well met," I said with a smile when I reached Ida. I found it funny that we both favoured the same café of all the cafés there. We stepped away from the door to be able to talk uninterrupted.

"Are we becoming BFFs?" she quizzed me with a grin. "You've contacted me twice in two days."

I tried to smile, but remembering why I'd contacted her made it look more like a grimace. "It might be this is actually the last time we meet."

Laughter disappeared from her eyes. "Oh?"

"Your cousin broke off the engagement with mine this morning."

"What?" She made a sharp, rejecting gesture with her hand. "That's not possible."

"He did. He even made her give the ring back. Olivia is distraught." I didn't want to tell her about Henry's claim that he didn't remember Olivia, that was too incredible, but I had to tell her something. "I think it's Jack's fault."

She pulled back. "What does he have to do with it?"

"I … had an altercation with him last night and he didn't take it well. He threatened Olivia, and now this. I think he talked Henry into breaking up with her."

"I told you he's no good."

"You did," I admitted, even though she'd talked about womanising and didn't know about the rest. "Could you talk with Henry? Or Jack?"

Her mouth tightened with determination. "Don't worry, I will."

Saved by the Spell

Relief released a knot in my gut. "Thank you. Let me know how it goes. I'm away the whole day with my boss, but send a message."

She tilted her head, looking over my shoulder. "Is that your boss?"

I turned to look and saw that Kane was waiting for me by the gallery with tense impatience. His suit was impeccable as always, his handsome face groomed, and his black hair settled for once. "Yes."

"Nice..."

"He is," I admitted with an easy smile. "But I guess I have to go before he comes to fetch me."

With a wave, I crossed the court to Kane, and we headed to his car.

"Will she be able to help?" he asked, glancing back at Ida, who had already returned to the café.

"She'll talk to Henry, and maybe Jack too."

One less worry for me.

Since Kane's Jag was in the shop having its tyres replaced, he'd driven to work in his other car, a large Land Cruiser with plenty of room at the back for transporting antique furniture and other items he collected from all around the country. It was old, its blue paint faded to grey, but there was much more room inside than in the luxurious Jaguar.

"Do you want me to sit in the back?" I asked, eyeing the back seat with misgiving. Years of being used as a furniture transport had made the upholstery and cushioning suffer and it didn't look terribly comfortable.

"It won't make much difference. I'll manage."

I climbed next to him. He set the address on the GPS, and we headed into the traffic.

"Do you think we should fetch Ashley?"

He gave me a puzzled glance. "What could she do against powerful mage?"

"I don't know, bite him?"

He grinned. "That would be a sight."

"She did manage to subdue the demon that attacked you," I pointed out. "In human form."

He swallowed, his mouth tightening, but he nodded. "True. Let's fetch her."

Ashley was instantly willing to participate, even though she had to sacrifice her day off for it, and so was Giselle. Soon the four of us were on our way to Blackhart's house.

"Do you think he'll be there?" Giselle asked. "Maybe he has a day job like a normal person."

"There isn't much more we can do," Kane reminded her.

"If we need to stake out the place, I can take today. Luca can take the night like the last time," Ashley promised. "But I'm back on duty tomorrow, so you'll have to take the next day."

"If we haven't found Rupert by tonight, I'm not sure there's much point in looking anymore," Giselle said grimly. We drove in silence after that.

The address was near Parliament Hill on the south side of Hampstead Heath. Streets rose steeply towards the top of the hill, with three-story redbrick Victorian terraces and houses on both sides. Hedge fund managers, media personalities, and other people with excellent incomes lived there.

Blackhart must be wealthy.

Mid-morning, the streets were relatively empty of cars, and we had no trouble finding a place to park, choosing a spot one street over. We exited the car and looked around.

Saved by the Spell

"Nothing immediately strikes me as magical around here," Kane noted. "Let's go take a closer look."

The street Blackhart lived on ran along the edge of the heath, the back gardens of the houses facing the park. His house was divided into several flats, and I went to check the names on the door to see which one belonged to him, while others waited by the street.

There was no Blackhart, but there was a familiar name. My heart jumped to my throat, and I had difficulty swallowing.

Jack Palmer.

Fourteen

"WHY WOULD DANIELLE LIE TO US?" Kane asked, looking a bit hurt, when I told them who lived there.

I gave him a pointed look. "Apart from the obvious?" But he wasn't amused, so I shrugged. "Maybe Blackhart lied to her. I wouldn't wonder it. Or he lives with Jack."

"I seriously doubt *that*," Ashley noted, and I was inclined to agree. "So which flat belongs to the little shit?"

"The upmost," I told her, and she nodded.

"I'll round the house to check it from the back."

She headed to the park with a steady lope, and the rest of us retreated away from the door so that we wouldn't be instantly spotted if Jack happened to exit the building.

"What now?" Giselle asked. "Shall we stay here and keep an eye on the place?"

"Is Jack home?" I asked Kane, who shook his head.

"The spell isn't reacting to him at all. It has a fairly wide range too, so I'd say he's not anywhere near."

"In that case, this would be the best time to sneak into his flat to look for the spell book," I suggested, but like before, he rejected it instantly.

"Absolutely not! And what if Blackhart is there?"

It was a worrying possibility, but I couldn't let that stop me. I needed the book. "There's four of us. What could he do?"

"Plenty," Kane said, but Giselle gave me a pensive nod.

"This is the only chance we have. What if we don't find Rupert in time."

Two against one, Kane gave up. "Fine, but I want Ashley with us."

I dug out my mobile and called her, and she soon returned. "We're breaking into Jack's flat," I told her, and she was instantly excited.

"Excellent. I can keep watch."

Now that we were doing this, I was getting nervous. I'd never done anything criminal before, and I was sure this was the first time for my companions too. Experience was needed in these kinds of undertakings, and we were sadly lacking.

Kane studied the entrance door carefully, running his hand above it as if feeling the air, and found three different wards on it. "I can't take all these down, or they'll know instantly that we're here."

"We'll look for another way in, then," Giselle declared, heading down the steps to round the house.

We found a small annex at the end of the house that led below grounds. Since the basement flat had its own entrance towards the street, we concluded that this one was for the rest of the house to use. And it only had one simple ward on it that Kane quickly took down.

Another feat of magic opened the lock, and we were in.

Saved by the Spell

It was a small storage space for bicycles and garden tools, and there was no alarm—which we came to think of only belatedly. Concrete steps led up into the house, and the door at the top opened to the entrance hall. It was a small, later addition when the one-family house had been converted into flats.

A narrow staircase led up on one side, and we climbed the slightly worn wooden steps as quietly as we could, with Kane checking for wards on each landing. But Jack—or Blackhart—hadn't been so paranoid that he would've put obstacles or warning wards along the way.

On the other hand, there were several wards on the landing outside Jack's door. "These will take a moment to unravel," Kane said, studying them with grim determination.

"I'll help," Giselle offered. Together they began to take them down, working in concert, as if they'd done this before. Since I couldn't see the wards, I had nothing else to do than send updates to Ashley, who had found a spot up the street where to keep an eye on the house.

The wards came down faster than I'd imagined, and soon Kane had the door open. He checked the threshold for traps, but there were none. He listened carefully, but if there was someone in the flat, they weren't making any noise. Relaxing a little, he entered the flat.

"For the record, I don't usually break and enter into people's homes," he said in a quiet tone. Since this was the first time for Giselle and me too, we just nodded. I drew a deep breath before I stepped over the doorstep.

I was now officially a criminal.

Turned out, it was easier than I'd thought to break the law. My palms were getting a bit damp and my heart was beating too fast. But that was just for fear.

I paused to look around. It was a loft convert, a vast open space with no partitions, which allowed us to see pretty much everything with one glance. Only the loo was behind walls by the entrance, but there was a large bathtub in the middle of the bedroom area. Handy for watching TV while you bathed.

"Nice…" Giselle said, walking in deeper.

I nodded. The floors were polished oak, the walls plain redbrick, and the ceiling had the heavy support beams visible. Windows in the slanted ceiling gave in plenty of light. Furniture was a carefully selected combination of antique and modern that made my gallerist fingers itch.

It infuriated me to no end that Jack would live in such a beautiful home.

"Let's be fast," Kane said. None of us wanted to be surprised by Jack—or Blackhart.

With everything out in the open, it was a straightforward job to go through the flat. At first I was hesitant to rummage through the drawers, but urgency soon cured me of any scruples. And it turned out to be a quick job.

"Here!"

Giselle stood by the Super King size bed, holding a large leatherbound tome with both hands. Even knowing that Jack had stolen the book, I was slightly surprised that it was here.

"Shall we take it with us or just photograph the pertinent chapters?" she asked, opening the book to see that it truly was the one we wanted.

"We'll take it with us," Kane stated. "I don't care if he notices it's gone. It belongs to the library, and he stole it first. Let's go."

Saved by the Spell

We'd reached the door when my phone rang. "Palmer is approaching the house."

Everyone tensed. We looked around frantically, but there was nowhere for us to go, and nowhere in the flat to hide. Only one set of stairs led up to Jack's flat.

"Shall I stop him?" Ashley asked, but Kane shook his head.

"No, let him come up."

I gave him a wide-eyed stare, but he exited the flat calmly, closing the door behind us. With a couple of gestures, he replaced the wards he and Giselle had taken quite some time to unravel.

Handy.

Instead of heading down, he took a stance in front of the door, holding the book securely against his side. It didn't take long for Jack's steps to approach. In a few moments, he appeared on the landing below us. He glanced up, and stumbled to a halt.

"What the fuck?"

Kane showed him the book. "I'm taking this back."

"You broke into my home?"

"Feel free to take the matter to the police," Kane said with a sneer.

Anger marred Jack's handsome features and he squeezed his hand into a fist. When he opened it again, there was a ball of blue fire on it. My heart jumped in fright.

"You'd torch your own home just to get to us?"

"Might be worth it."

"Let me remind you that you can't attack me," Kane said, sounding amazingly calm.

"I can always attack the women."

Kane straightened, his muscles tensing. I could practically feel his anger brushing against my skin. I'd seen his temper, but never this furious.

"You do that ... and I'll end you."

The threat was the more terrifying for how calmly he delivered it. Jack ground his teeth together, but the fireball disappeared.

"It seems we're at impasse," he said. "I can't let you descend these steps with the book, and you're blocking the entrance to my home."

A growl reverberated from the stairs below him, making the small hairs in my body shoot up in primal fear. Jack jumped around, almost tripping. Ashley—or the wolf that she'd become—stepped onto the landing, snarling.

Jack retreated to the corner, slowly sinking down against the wall, leaning tightly to it as if making sure the wolf couldn't get him from behind, his knees curled in front of him to block the soft parts of his stomach.

Kane nodded. "We'll be leaving, then."

My legs weren't as steady as they could've been when I followed Kane down the stairs, past Jack who was staring at us with eyes so wide the whites stood out.

I couldn't resist a sneer at him, although I had to steel my spine to slip past Ashley. I knew it was her, but the sheer size of the wolf made me fear for my life. It didn't help that she snarled at us too when we slinked past.

I didn't pause until I was back on the street again. My shoulders slumped in relief and my knees were tottery.

"That went ... well."

Kane looked grim. "It wasn't flawless, but we got what we came here for. I'll go get the car."

It took me a moment to figure out why we couldn't just walk there. We couldn't let a bloody big wolf wander

Saved by the Spell

around a residential neighbourhood in the middle of the day.

Good thing we hadn't taken the Jag. She would never have fit in it in her current form.

Then again, she wouldn't have properly fit in her human form either.

Giselle, braver than me, waited with Ashley in the hall, ready to hide her with magic, and to make sure Jack didn't sneak up on us. Although it was probably more for his safety than ours.

He might end up as Ashley's lunch if he surprised the wolf.

Kane brought the car over and opened the door to the back. Giselle let the wolf out, following with her clothes, as Ashley hurried into the car. Kane closed the door behind her firmly.

We sighed collectively in relief when the wolf settled down on the floor of the boot. "We'd best get her home," Giselle said. "It'll take a while before she'll be able to shift back at this time of day when it's not even full moon."

"But we need to stay to keep an eye on the house," I pointed out, and Kane gave me a questioning look.

"Do you think Blackhart will come here?"

I shook my head. "I don't think he lives here. There were no signs of another resident in Jack's flat."

Giselle nodded. "Only Jack's."

"But Jack might lead us to Blackhart," I continued, "Or he might visit."

Kane looked like he would argue, but Giselle made the decision for him. "I'll take Ashley and the book home and return for you later."

With that, she climbed behind the wheel and was soon driving down the street, leaving us staring after the car.

He shot me an amused look. "I guess we're on a stakeout, then."

~ ~ ~

A STAKEOUT ON A RESIDENTIAL STREET would have been much easier if we'd had a car to wait in. There was nothing to hide behind, nothing to sit on. In our business clothes, we didn't look out of place—unless you wondered why we were loitering on the street—but they weren't exactly suitable for sculking in the bushes.

Not that there were bushes on this side of the house to sculk in. All the greenery had been saved for the back garden.

"How about the cellar?" I finally suggested. "We can keep an eye on the hallway from the steps if we crack the door there open."

Kane opened the lock on the basement door with magic again, and soon we were climbing the concrete steps to the door that separated the cellar from the entrance hall. They were narrow and there was no room for the two of us, even if one of us hadn't been spelled to repulse the other.

"Let's take turns. I'll take the first one."

The relief on Kane's face when he could retreat to the bottom of the steps really irked me. Maybe because we weren't any closer to breaking the spell.

"I'd like to assure you that criminal activities aren't considered part of your duties," he said, sitting down on the bottom step, trying to find a comfortable position for his long legs. It would've been easier for him to sit on an upper step, but that would've brought him too close to me.

Saved by the Spell

"This is a one-time exception and I'm sorry you were dragged into it."

"Again," I noted dryly. "So does that mean I won't be paid for today's work?"

The corners of his eyes crinkled as he grinned. "I would be a bad employer if I made you do burglary for free."

I grinned too, happy that he wasn't angry that I'd forced him this far out of his comfort zone.

"Maybe I could add this in my resumé as a skill…"

His mouth quirked. "Considering I did all the breaking and entering, you would be falsely advertising."

"And you were good at it." I heaved a sigh. "It would be really handy to learn some of your skills. Are you sure a mundane like me can't be taught?"

"I'm afraid not." He made a commiserating face. "The inner ability to manipulate the physics has to be there."

Since he'd recently ended a secret society run by mages, i.e. Danielle and Blackhart, who were conning humans into thinking they could learn magic, I let the matter be.

He took out his phone and began to go through his emails. I took out mine too. Just because we weren't at the office didn't mean the work didn't need doing, but I had to keep an eye on the hallway and couldn't let my attention waver.

Nothing happened. Clearly everyone living here had somewhere to be during the day, and no one was home. There were no deliveries, or even a mailman making rounds. I was bored before an hour had gone by, and my bottom was starting to go numb on the cold step.

I stood up to stretch my legs and get the blood flowing again.

"Do you want to switch?"

My attention on the door, Kane's voice right behind me made me jump. My leg slipped and I would have fallen down the stairs if he hadn't managed to wrap his arms around me.

I clung to him, my heart beating in fright. He held me tightly, momentarily ignoring how sick I made him, until an involuntary shudder ran through him. Reluctantly, I detached myself.

"Thanks." My voice was breathless. "I was just stretching my legs."

He studied me, his blue eyes full of concern. "I don't mind taking a turn."

I could have continued my watch, but he clearly wanted to switch places, so I nodded.

I turned to descend the stairs—carefully—when the front door buzzed, indicating that the lock was being remotely opened.

We froze, unable to breathe, as the front door was pushed open and someone walked in. My mouth dropped when I recognised her.

Ida.

She didn't glance in our direction but headed briskly up the stairs. We waited until we were sure she couldn't hear us before we let ourselves relax. We shared baffled stares.

"She really took the breakup to heart, if she's sacrificing her lunch for this," I said, pleased. "I hope she can talk some sense into Jack."

"It might be difficult, considering that his actions weren't caused by the young couple."

Saved by the Spell

He was right, but I held on to the hope. I didn't care all that much about Olivia's happiness, but she could make my life difficult if things didn't go her way.

"Mind you, my life would be a tad less complicated if the wedding stayed off," I noted, remembering what I'd meant to tell him earlier. His brows shot up.

"How so?"

"The wedding was supposed to be held the day we have the auction."

He blinked. Then the corner of his mouth curled up in amusement. "I'm sure we could've managed just with Mrs Walsh this once."

My dismay on his careless dismissal of my importance must have shown, because he laughed and pulled me into a hug—a real, spontaneous show of ... I don't know, affection? Amusement?

It ended before it had properly begun, because of the spell—and because he suddenly remembered we didn't hug. He cleared his throat, acutely awkward, like only a proper Englishman could be.

"Sorry about that."

"No problem," I said, breathless again, but not for fright this time. When Kane forgot to behave like a Victorian gentleman, he was really ... charming.

The sounds of two people approaching down the stairs startled us to action. Kane closed the door to the hallway and pointed at me to descend to the cellar, following right behind me. We hurried out and were peering around the corner of the house when Jack and Ida exited.

They were talking animatedly about something, but neither of them looked angry or disappointed. Maybe their discussion had gone well, short though it had been.

Fingers crossed.

Jack walked Ida across the street to her car—or maybe it was his, because he gave her the key. He held the door open for her, but they stood there talking for a few more minutes.

Then she reached up, and he wrapped his arms around her waist, pulling her tightly against his body. And then they kissed.

Passionately.

Fifteen

MY LEGS LOST THEIR INTEGRITY AND I leaned heavily against Kane, not caring whether he could handle it or not.

"I did not see that coming…"

I fought to keep the contents of my stomach down, though I don't know why. I wasn't in love with Jack. I wasn't even attracted to him anymore. He could kiss whomever he wanted.

But Ida…

I had thought she was sincere with me when she warned me about Jack. She hadn't indicated in any way that she might be interested in him, let alone deeply involved with him.

Why would she do that? What game was she playing?

Kane cleared his throat. "I'm sorry."

That brought me back to my surroundings enough to stand on my own legs. He was getting better at not showing his revulsion, but I could see the lines around his mouth ease when I stepped away.

"It's not about Jack," I explained. "I'd sort of thought Ida could be my friend. But she kept this to herself.

Allowed him to flirt with me at the engagement party and didn't comment at all when I went out with him. And why did he ask me out if he's with her?"

Other than that he truly was a womaniser. But what sort of a woman watched from the side and encouraged such behaviour?

I know what my reaction had been when I learned Troy had been cheating on me.

Kane patted me on the shoulder, a bit clumsily. "I'm sorry about that, then."

Ida and Jack ended the kiss. She got into the car and drove away, leaving him standing there, staring after the retreating vehicle. He had not looked at me with such longing, not even to pretend he was interested in me.

When the car had disappeared around the corner, he visibly shook himself. Then he headed resolutely up the street and turned towards the heath at the corner.

"Let's follow," I said to Kane, already going after him.

"What if he's going for a jog?" he asked, catching up with me.

"Dressed like that?"

Jack was wearing the same business casual as when we'd encountered him in the hallway, jeans and a blazer with a chequered shirt. His leather Oxfords most assuredly weren't meant for running.

I wouldn't necessarily go for a walk in them either.

"He might be headed to Henry's," I said. "The family lives at the north-western edge of the heath."

Whatever Ida had said to him must have been effective to get him to act immediately—and on foot, since he'd given her his car.

There were no trees blocking the view and we could easily see Jack, leisurely walking up the hill. But he wasn't

Saved by the Spell

heading to where the Sanfords lived. He was walking towards the viewpoint at the top of the Parliament Hill.

"Why's he heading there?" Kane asked bewildered.

"Instagram photos?" I suggested, half in jest, but I wondered the same. "Maybe he's just crossing the heath."

He shot me a sidelong look. "What could possibly draw him at the other side?"

I wasn't familiar with Hampstead Heath, despite having climbed to the viewpoint myself a couple of times to watch London stretch below me. I took out my phone, opened the map app, and we paused to study it; we could see Jack from afar, and Kane had the spell tracking him too.

"He could still take another path north," I said, but I didn't really believe it, as it would be an odd detour. "Maybe he's off to play tennis." There were tennis courts on the eastern edge of the heath.

"Wouldn't he be carrying some sort of equipment bag in that case?" Kane asked. But there were other possibilities.

"There are several restaurants and pubs on Highgate Road. Maybe he's meeting Henry in one of them."

"Or Blackhart."

My heart jumped. I put the phone away and we followed Jack at a brisker pace, Kane's considerably brisker than mine, thanks to his longer legs.

"What if he's keeping tabs on me with his tracking spell and knows we're here?" We were far enough behind him that even if he turned to look, he wouldn't recognise us, but a spell was different.

"Do you feel the pressure on your neck?"

"No."

"Then I'd say the chance is remote. And it's not like we have a choice."

The heath was large and there were a lot of people around, enjoying the day. Jack didn't pause to speak with anyone, but headed resolutely down the hill to its east side, exiting onto Highgate Road. Hedges lined the park, blocking our view, and we hurried to catch up.

"I sense him continuing straight forward," Kane said as we reached the street. We looked around and spotted Jack on the other side of the busy street heading towards the residential area east of the heath. "There are no restaurants in that direction."

"Maybe Blackhart lives there?" I suggested.

"Or someone wholly unrelated to this business," Kane noted dryly, but he didn't slow down. For a boring antiques dealer, he was really entering into the spirit of sleuthing.

The street turned uphill again, and despite my newly begun spin classes, I was starting to feel the strain of the long walk. To make matters worse, the fabulous leather boots that I loved turned out to pinch my feet when used for actual walking.

And still Jack went on.

A vast park spread on the right side of the street, and I hoped Jack wasn't on a trek through local green spaces. It looked vaguely familiar, but it wasn't until I spotted a large crypt that I recognised where we were.

"That's Highgate Cemetery!"

It was a huge old place, with Victorian crypts and celebrity tombs, though I only knew Douglas Adams and Karl Marx. It was a tourist attraction and a nature reserve, a wild, beautiful place even in autumn, the foliage turning gold and red.

Saved by the Spell

The gatehouse, a large limestone building from the 1830s, was further up the street on the western side, which was the older half of the cemetery. Under our baffled watch, Jack headed straight there.

"I did not see this coming," Kane said, slowing down while Jack showed something at the gate and walked in.

"I thought the place was only open on weekends," I mused. "Or with guided tours."

We walked closer and a sign informed us that the East Cemetery was open every day, but the West Cemetery was open only for those who had family graves there.

Jack apparently did.

"I didn't take him for a familial fellow."

Kane's eyes tightened at the corners as he studied the gatehouse. "Maybe something else is going on. Come on."

He walked to the ticket booth and purchased us tickets to the East Cemetery. I didn't demur and offer to pay mine. It was only four pounds, and I was here because of magic trouble.

I also didn't point out that Jack had headed to the West Cemetery, because one couldn't buy tickets there today.

We were given a map and offered a guided tour, which we declined. Calmly, like a pair of tourists, we walked through the gate and down the path that would lead to an underpass to the East Cemetery. Once out of sight of the ticket booth, we paused to read the map.

"This isn't at all helpful," I said, studying it annoyed.

It listed the most important attractions in the West Cemetery, like the Terrace Catacombs and Egyptian Avenue, and the most notable graves, but the ordinary people weren't mentioned.

"How are we supposed to find which way Jack went if we don't know what grave he's visiting?"

"Luckily, the spell tells me where he is," Kane said.

He glanced around, but we were the only people there. His mouth pursed in a determined line, he drew a fortifying breath and pulled me flush against his side, wrapping an arm around me.

My breath caught in surprise. A whiff of his cologne reached my nose, and I felt a flush creep up my spine. Having him hold me so close, so unexpectedly, was truly unnerving and kind of … exhilarating.

But not as unnerving as what happened next.

He made a series of gestures with his hands that I'd come to associate with his ward-casting—as opposed to spell work that required chanting and chalk circles. Small hairs in my body shot up as magic wrapped around me more intimately than he did.

"We are now sort of invisible, but it only lasts for a few moments," he said in a low voice. "Come on."

Not waiting for my answer, he walked me to the gate that led to West Cemetery. He glanced around, but we were still alone. He pulled me close, my back pressing against his chest, his arms wrapped around my torso, and pushed us through the turnstile.

It was a tight fit, as we had to use the same slot, but we made it. If anyone noticed the stile turn on its own, they didn't come to investigate.

"Hurry," he murmured against my ear, pushing me down the path. The moment we were hidden by the ever-present wilderness, he stopped. With an audible sigh of relief, he pulled away from me.

I shivered, mostly in cold. Not that the day was chilly.

Saved by the Spell

"The ward held better than I hoped, even with the two of us," he said, pleased, impervious to my flustered state. Then he checked the invisible spell tracking Jack and pointed down the path we were on.

"This way."

Jack had a good head start, but the magic pulled Kane to the right direction. The paths didn't always lead to where he wanted to go though, and a few times we had to consult the map to find the best route.

In normal conditions, I would have enjoyed the walk in the beautiful cemetery, the wildly growing greenery that filled the space between the tombs and the calming sounds of nature around us. But I barely noticed my surroundings as I hurried next to him, trying to keep up with his long strides.

And then he abruptly stopped. I ground to a halt, the gravel sliding under my boots.

"He disappeared." He swirled around, looking annoyed. "I can't sense him anywhere."

"What does that mean?" I looked around too, as if Jack would somehow be visible to my eyes. "Could he have entered one of the crypts?"

"I'd still sense him. The spell has a good range. But it can't find him anymore."

"So he hasn't left the cemetery either?"

He gestured with his arms. "He must have. With a jet engine, probably," he huffed, aggravated. "I don't see how else he could've disappeared so fast."

I bit my lower lip as I tried to come up with a different explanation. I stiffened when a thought hit me.

"Or he has noticed the tracking spell and blocked it somehow."

~ ~ ~

Kane's hair billowed as a sign of his frustrated anger, only to settle down immediately. "No, it's not possible to block the spell on the fly, even if he has noticed it."

I'd imagined Jack wrapping himself in tinfoil, but apparently not.

"Maybe he realised the spell is there when we broke into his house, and prepared a counter-spell at home?"

His eyes narrowed. "I guess that's possible, although mine doesn't create a pressure on the person being tracked, so he shouldn't sense it. But why wait until here to activate it?"

"To lure us away from where he really wants to go?"

"Or to make sure we're not there to witness when Blackhart visits him," he countered.

"Blast." I'd walked all this way for nothing.

He turned and stalked back the way we'd come with long strides. I hurried after him. "Shouldn't we check the cemetery anyway?"

He glanced at me but didn't slow down. "Why? He's blocked the spell and slipped away. He could be anywhere. We'd best return to his house to see who'll visit him."

It made sense, but I wasn't convinced.

"But why would he have chosen here of all places to do so? He could've taken the Tube and led us pretty much anywhere on a wild goose chase, and much easier and faster."

He paused so abruptly I almost collided with him, and had to steady myself by his upper arm. He was so focused on my rebuttal that he didn't even notice—or at least didn't step away from me.

"You're right. So why did he come here…?"

Saved by the Spell

I looked around at the rows of old crypts that rose from the foliage as if they'd grown there, the stone on the walls so worn one couldn't read the names on them anymore, and the angel and lion statues guarding them. Even in the daylight, the place had interesting atmosphere.

"Could they have a secret lair here?" I asked.

His brows shot up. "That's spooky."

"It fits my notion of an evil mage perfectly," I argued, shuddering. "Okay, how about secret tunnels, then? The hill must be riddled with them."

He nodded. "There are the catacombs, but I don't think they really lead anywhere."

"Let's check them anyway. Maybe Jack's underground somewhere and that's why you can't sense him anymore."

He opened his mouth as if to argue, but reconsidered and opened the map to check the fastest route.

The Terrace Catacombs stood on the highest point of the cemetery in the erstwhile garden of a manor house that had been demolished when the cemetery was built in 1830s. It was a wide and tall wall built into the side of the hill. The façade was limestone, with dozens of iron doors to private crypts side by side, separated by half-columns and other architectural features.

A wrought iron gate in the middle led into a vaulted brick gallery inside the structure, over eighty yards long. It had recesses on both sides just large enough to hold a coffin, stacked from floor to ceiling like pigeonholes.

The gate was locked, but that didn't stop Kane. It opened silently, and closed behind us with a clank. It was cool inside, but not gloomy, as light poured in from the round holes in the ceiling. We walked to the end, but there was nothing there, no hidden doors and no mages hiding in the coffin holes. I could see, because there were no hatches covering the ancient, decaying coffins.

A shiver ran down my spine.

We retreated outside, and looked over the cemetery stretching at our feet, but trees blocked most of the view. Jack could be down there and we wouldn't spot him.

I studied the terrace structure, the limestone wall, and the private catacombs. "How about one of these?" I suggested, pointing at the iron doors. "Maybe the Palmer family crypt is in one of these."

It was a long shot, but this was the only place with potential for an underground tunnel.

Since the gate was in the middle of the structure, I headed in one direction and Kane to the other, checking each door. Some of the names had disappeared almost completely, but what letters were visible didn't look like Palmer—or Blackhart either for that matter. I wasn't ready to give up the idea that he had his lair here.

I reached the second to last door and paused, my insides turning cold.

"I think I found it," I said to Kane, raising my voice just a little so that he could hear it at the other end.

He hurried to me and was soon staring at the door I indicated. "I don't understand. That's not Palmer."

"No, it's Sanford. The crypt belongs to Henry's family."

And Ida's.

He nodded, understanding. "Do you think Henry is involved after all? Or that Jack is taking advantage of the family's crypt?"

I had no idea what I thought, but this couldn't be a coincidence.

"Or Blackhart is."

Saved by the Spell

He tilted his head in acknowledgement and reached for the handle on the iron plate door.

A wall of light flashed, bright even in daylight, and a wave of invisible energy bolted him backwards with force.

He landed on his back several yards away and lay on the lawn, unconscious.

Sixteen

I RUSHED TO HIM AND KNELT BY his head. "Kane!" My heart was beating in fright and my hands were shaking as I reached to feel his pulse. Tears of relief sprang into my eyes when I felt it.

I patted him lightly on the cheek. "Kane. Archibald."

Not even using his given name roused him. I bit my lip, unable to decide what I should do.

I should call an ambulance, but we were here unauthorised. It would be difficult to explain our presence. And it would be impossible to tell what had happened to him. "Well, you see, there was this magical barrier on the door that repulsed him with such force it stunned him…"

That would go well.

I took out my phone and called Giselle. "Are you anywhere near Highgate Cemetery yet?"

We'd updated her on our location earlier, and she'd promised to come and fetch us.

"No, I'm still at home. Ashley's shift drained her completely and she needs watching over."

"Shit."

My tears began to fall, and I had to swallow to unblock my throat.

"What's wrong?"

It took an effort to speak. "Kane triggered a ward of some sort and now he's unconscious and I can't wake him up."

"Oh my God. Are you still at the cemetery?"

"Yes. We found where Jack disappeared to, and were about to follow, when Kane triggered the ward."

He'd been so careful checking the wards in Jack's flat. Why hadn't he done so here? Then another thought hit.

"What if Jack returns and finds us here?" I was defenceless without magic. "What if Blackhart finds us here? He could hurt Kane. Or worse…"

It was such a frightening idea that it dried my tears. I looked frantically around for a place to hide us in, but the only suitable place close enough I could access was the catacomb gallery. If we went deep enough down it we wouldn't be spotted from the outside.

"I'll have to move him to a shelter. Can you get here, fast?"

"I'll come as soon as I can," Giselle promised, ending the call before I remembered to tell her that she'd have to use magical stealth because the place wasn't open.

She'd figure it out.

I rushed to open the gate that Kane luckily had left unlocked after our brief visit. Returning to him, I tried to revive him once more, but there was no reaction.

I was beginning to worry in earnest. The longer he was unconscious, the more severe the trauma.

I slipped a hand behind his neck and felt the back of his head. There was no blood, and I couldn't feel a lump

Saved by the Spell

even, so it wasn't a blow to his head that kept him unconscious. It had to be the ward that caused this.

I considered his prone body, trying to figure out the best way to move him. He was tall and slim, but with defined muscles. He was probably heavy.

But I had to move him, so I took a hold under his arms and began to drag him. I couldn't help remembering the times I'd had to move my old flatmate Nick every time he'd passed out somewhere—like in the shower.

At least Kane was fully clothed. More's the pity.

It turned out that a naked man on a wet tile floor was much easier to move than a besuited man on grass and gravel. Inch by slow inch I dragged him towards the crypt. My back soon ached, the bent position not exactly ergonomic, and the muscles in my thighs burned.

It was only forty yards, but it felt endless. By the time I reached the catacomb, I was sweaty and breathless. The moment I deemed we were deep enough into the gallery, I placed him carefully down and collapsed next to him, panting in exhaustion.

His phone rang and I shrieked, the sound echoing in the vaults. Most embarrassing.

With shaking hands, I dug into the inside breast pocket of his suit in case it was a client trying to reach him. And why hadn't he kept the phone switched off anyway? We were on a stealth mission.

When I saw who it was, I wish I hadn't bothered.
Danielle.

I considered briefly not answering, but she could have vital information about Blackhart that would help us find Rupert.

But since it wasn't a video call, I decided to pretend I didn't know who was calling. "Kane's Art and Antiques, Phoebe Thorpe speaking."

"Why are you answering Archie's phone?" Danielle asked archly.

"I'm sorry, who is this?"

I could swear she was growling, and I thought it best not to aggravate her further.

"Danielle? Are you calling about Blackhart?"

"I'm only speaking with Archie."

I glanced at the unconscious figure next to me, spreadeagled on the floor, his suit coat rumpled and likely ruined. "I'm afraid it's not possible right now."

"Look, girl, I don't know who you are, and what you think you mean to Archibald, but you will not stop me from speaking with him."

Bitch.

"You'll have to wait for him to become available, then."

"Is he in the loo?" she asked in a fed-up tone like only a wife could. Or an ex-wife.

"No, he's unconscious."

I don't know why I said it, but it had the satisfying effect of silencing her. Completely. I don't know if she'd ever been that speechless before. I had to check the phone display to see that the call was still connected.

"Tell me what happened," she finally demanded, but her voice lacked the angry strength of earlier.

I wasn't cruel enough to keep her in the dark. "We tracked Jack to what we think is Blackhart's hiding place and he was dumb enough not to check the door for wards first."

"Where are you?"

Saved by the Spell

"Why?"

"Where?" she demanded, more forcefully. I rolled my eyes, but answered.

"In the Terrace Catacombs of Highgate Cemetery."

"Show me."

I resented being given such curt orders, but I opened the video display and showed her around, including Kane's still figure on the floor. Her mouth tightened into a line, but she didn't say anything.

"Don't move."

As if I had energy to do anything but sit on the dirty floor.

She ended the call without a word, and I rolled my eyes again. It was either that or start crying.

I'd barely put Kane's phone back in his pocket, when deeper into the gallery the air began to shimmer, like a mirage that reached from floor to ceiling.

At first, I thought my tired eyes were deceiving me, but in a few heartbeats the gallery disappeared completely, revealing a room with bland walls and no furniture.

A portal!

Before my horrified gaze, Laurent Dufort stepped out, followed by Danielle.

~ ~ ~

I THREW MYSELF OVER KANE, as if that would help against magic. "You will not harm him!" I shrieked, fear making my voice reedy.

The portal disappeared, and Dufort sneered, amused, but to my frightened eyes it seemed sinister. "Relax, we're here to help."

It sounded charming in is French accent, but I wasn't about to let my guard down. "You're not touching him. I know what you are, *warlock.*"

I spat the last word with as much venom as I could. Danielle huffed and stepped closer. I threw my hand up, palm towards her. "You're not any better. You tried to kill me."

"And you cursed me," she countered.

"You cursed me first."

Dufort held his hands up in a calming fashion. "Ladies, why don't we concentrate on the essential. Monsieur Kane has been injured by a ward, *non?*"

I shot him a wary look, not about to let my guard down just because he sounded reasonable. "I don't know what it was. It's on the crypt door left from the gate, the one that says Sanford."

He nodded and headed out of the gate. Danielle crouched on the other side of Kane, but wisely didn't touch him. "How long has he been unconscious?"

"Maybe fifteen minutes." In truth, I had no idea, but it had taken a while to drag him here.

"What happened to his clothes?" she asked, appalled. She knew as well as I did how fastidious he was about his looks.

"I had to drag him here, didn't I, in case Blackhart arrived and attacked him." I sounded defensive, even though it was a perfectly valid reason.

She sneered. "Pity you're not one of us. There's a handy levitation spell for moving heavy objects."

Her tone indicated that I was vastly inferior creature, but before I managed a suitable response, Dufort returned.

Saved by the Spell

"That was a nasty ward on the door. Black magic, almost warlock quality. Lucky I was here, or you would've needed the blood of the caster to take them down. Or the caster himself."

My stomach lurched. "Has Blackhart crossed that line?" I asked Danielle, who shrugged.

"He hadn't a month ago."

A lot could happen in a month, especially if your grand scheme of taking over the world by using unsuspecting humans had been spoiled.

"He hasn't ... killed Rupert, has he?"

"He'd have done it at his home, not dragged him around London," she said, sounding impatient. "Besides, the sacrifice doesn't have to be a powerful person for him to cross the line."

"You would know…"

Her eyes flashed in anger, but before she could retaliate, Dufort spoke: "Monsieur Kane's state is caused by the ward, and you cannot wake him up by ordinary means. You need my help."

I faced him. "What's the price?"

"As if you wouldn't pay it," Danielle sneered, but I kept my eyes on Dufort's. Their strength was more than I could easily bear, but I endured. His mouth quirked.

"No charge. This time."

"So you're like drug dealers," I said, disgusted. "First time's free and then the price goes up exponentially."

To my surprise, he laughed. Evil people had a weird sense of humour.

And a charming laugh.

"You helped my Danielle with the curse. Consider this a debt repaid."

He'd sent a hellhound to kill her, but whatever. It wasn't my relationship.

I made a sweeping gesture at Kane. "Proceed, then. But I'm keeping an eye on you. And there had better not be any evil consequences, or I'll come after you with a vengeance."

He laughed again and gestured me to move back. My legs had stiffened, and it took a moment to get them to obey, but I managed to retreat a little.

I wouldn't go farther than that.

He placed a hand on Kane's forehead and listened—or studied him with the third eye or whatever. I'm not an expert on warlock healing.

His dark brows furrowed, and he shot me a look. "I need your blood."

"What?"

"Would you rather I use mine?"

"No…?"

He held out a hand and, reluctantly, I reached mine to him. His hand was large and warm around mine, which surprised me a little. I guess I thought he would be cold. Evil should be.

He studied my hand. "I presume there's a reason why you feel repulsive to me?"

"Yes."

My curt answer made him smile. He didn't seem as strained by the revulsion as other men were, and held my hand with ease. Perhaps warlocks were more immune to the effects, or he could shield himself against them.

Or he was simply so cool that he didn't care.

A triumphant smile flashed on Danielle's face, and I had a suspicion she knew exactly how the spell had come to be. She'd been in London back when Jack had stolen

Saved by the Spell

the book. She could have been the cloaked mage with him!

I don't know why I hadn't come to think of that before.

There was a small prick in my index finger, and I startled, more out of surprise than pain because he hadn't used any tool.

Blood welled at the tip. He waited a couple of heartbeats, and then, using my finger like a pen, drew a symbol on Kane's forehead. He didn't stir.

My blood looked grotesque on his pale skin, and I found the drawing difficult to look at, as if it were repelling me. It was evil if anything was.

I was starting to question the wisdom of this. But Dufort was the only one who could help.

Dufort released my hand, and I sucked the finger to stop the blood flowing. Danielle shook her head, disgusted, reached into Kane's breast pocket and pulled out the fine muslin handkerchief he always had there. She handed it to me without a word, and I wrapped it around the wound, even though it would be ruined.

Then again, considering the condition of his suit, one ruined hankie wouldn't make matters much worse.

Dufort concentrated on Kane, ignoring us. He didn't move or gesture with his hands, but I felt power rising, the magic brushing against me. It felt different from Kane's. Kane's made my skin tingle pleasantly, but this was a harsher sensation. Forceful and raw, not at all as charming as he was.

He placed a hand above the symbol he'd drawn and said a word that my ears refused to hear. The effect was immediate.

Kane's chest arched up, like in the movies when they use a defibrillator to start someone's heart, and he drew a loud breath as if he hadn't been breathing the whole time, though I knew he had.

His eyes opened, and he stared up in confusion. Then he shot to a sitting position, punched Dufort in the face, and promptly lost consciousness again, collapsing back on the floor.

That went well.

Seventeen

SPEECHLESS, I GAVE THE HANDKERCHIEF to Dufort, and he used it to dab the blood from his lip. It was only a nick, as Kane had been too dazed to do proper damage, and it stopped bleeding instantly.

Danielle looked bewildered. "He's never been violent before."

"Effects of the spell, I'm afraid," Dufort said in French, brushing her words aside. He didn't look angry.

I had a different theory. Kane had been really worried about Danielle, fearing she was being abused by Dufort. This wasn't his violent side we'd witnessed; it was his chivalric self.

I thought it best not to bring it up.

"Will he be unconscious for long?" I asked, worried, opting to speak English even though my French was rather good, thanks to my parents living there for so long.

Dufort made a very Gallic shrug. "Impossible to tell, but at least it's not caused by magic anymore, so if it continues, you can take him to a doctor."

The colour of Kane's skin was better, and he was breathing more evenly, so I decided to trust Dufort's assessment. To my amazement, the symbol he'd drawn on Kane's forehead was gone too, as if erased by the spell.

"Thank you." And I meant it too. Evil or not, he'd been helpful.

My phone vibrated in my pocket, startling me. Giselle called. "Where are you?"

I told her our location and she said they'd soon be here.

Dufort helped Danielle up, and held her hand after, gently caressing it. She didn't try to pull it away and she smiled at him, so I was almost confident she was with him voluntarily.

"I think that's the cue for us to leave," Dufort said with a small bow at me. "I've removed the most vicious wards off the door. Ordinary mages should be able to remove the rest."

He extended his arm in front of him and made a circle in the air with his open palm. A portal opened and they stepped through without a word—and before I could ask what he wanted in return for that other service.

I had a bad feeling we'd find out the hard way.

I hadn't recovered from their visit by the time Giselle arrived with Amber. They approached cautiously, peering in through the wrought iron gate.

"There you are."

Giselle's shoulders slumped in relief, and she rushed to us, Amber at her heels. The latter was carrying a bag full of what I hoped was medical aid to revive Kane.

"Has he been unconscious all this time?" Amber asked worried, kneeling by him to check his pulse.

"Sort of."

Saved by the Spell

She shot me a questioning look and I shrugged. "Laurent Dufort was here with Danielle, and he managed to revive him briefly."

Amber's mouth dropped open. "What?"

"Did he attack Archibald?" Giselle demanded, her normally smiling countenance wiped away with anger.

"No. He wanted to ... help him, I guess."

The women didn't look like they believed me, so I told them the bizarre story while Amber took care of Kane.

"I think you're right," Amber said once I'd finished. "He'll want a favour in return, and it's not going to be good."

I'd worry about that later.

Giselle took a bunch of herbs from the bag and lit them up. The smoke was pungent, and she held it under Kane's nose. His eyes opened immediately, and he coughed violently until the smoke cleared.

He studied them blearily. "How did you get here?" Then he lifted his head, wincing. "Where is here?"

"We're still in the catacombs," I told him.

I had a great urge to hold his hand, but I refrained, and not just because of the spell. He wouldn't welcome the gesture.

I could only watch as Giselle and Amber helped him to sit up. He swayed a little but didn't faint.

"You triggered a ward on the Sanford crypt and it knocked you out," I told him.

He rubbed his forehead, as if his head hurt. It probably did. "It's a really nasty ward I've never encountered before. I'm not sure I'll be able to break it."

"That's okay. Laurent Dufort already did."

"What?" His anger flared—as did his hair—and he made to get up, only to be held down by Amber's firm hand on his shoulder.

"How the hell did that happen?"

I spread my arms, still unable to believe the chain of events myself. "Danielle called you and I sort of blurted out you were unconscious. They stepped out of a portal a moment later."

His nostrils flared in disgust upon hearing about the portal. It was magic only warlocks could do.

"Anyway, he removed the nastiest wards, healed you, and then you punched him in the face."

"Really?" A satisfied smile spread on his face. "Pity I don't remember it."

"Let's hope he won't remember it either," Giselle said dryly. She leaned down and wrapped an arm under his. Amber took the other arm. "Let's get you up…"

Together, they helped him stand, and his legs held. He straightened his clothes, luckily not checking the state of his jacket—appalling—and nodded decisively. "Let's go find Rupert."

We didn't point out to him that he wasn't in any state to fight a warlock, or even a mage as powerful as an archmage. We'd manage somehow if it came to a confrontation.

But after studying the wards remaining on the door to the Sanford crypt, he had to admit defeat.

"Even without the black magic wards, this is a complicated piece of protection. It takes at least five people, preferably six, working in concert to break it, if you don't know the key that lets you pass."

Saved by the Spell

Giselle pursed her lips. "I don't know where we'll get more people at this hour. Ashley is incapacitated and Luca can't come before sundown."

She didn't say aloud that they didn't currently trust their fellow mages not to be in league with Blackhart, but that's what she meant. It was up to us to break the wards and find Rupert.

"We'll go home, recuperate and return with Luca," Amber stated. "And hopefully Ashley has recovered by then too."

As much as it worried me that we'd have to postpone finding Rupert, I couldn't help feeling relieved that we didn't have to go after Blackhart just yet, with Kane recovering. Amber and Giselle were clearly relieved too.

Kane looked like he wanted to argue, but Amber didn't give him a chance. She took him by the arm and led him down the path. He went with her with only a token protest.

She didn't head to the front gate but chose a path that led to a far corner on the same side. We ended up at a pair of tall iron gates wide enough to drive through with a car. They were held closed by a bicycle lock, and there were no cameras monitoring it.

That was trusting.

The street on the other side was empty, even though the residential neighbourhood began right outside the gate. Though it felt like hours had passed, it wasn't rush hour yet; people were still at work.

My stomach growled just then, reminding me that I hadn't eaten anything since breakfast, and then only a cup of coffee.

It was a matter of moment for the mages to open the lock and close it behind us. Soon, we were in Kane's car that the women had left on the next street over.

Kane fell asleep the moment the car was on the move, and we had to wake him up when we reached his home forty-five minutes later.

He promised to be at the House of Magic by dinner time, and we left him to make his own way indoors. But all three of us kept an eye on his progress like mother hens.

The moment he had disappeared into his house, Amber gave me a slow look. "What the hell happened to his clothes?"

~ ~ ~

I WAS RESTED AND WELL-FED by the time we filed back into Kane's Land Rover after sunset that evening, but I can't say I was relaxed. I sat on the edge of the back seat, holding myself rigid, until Giselle pulled me to lean against the backrest.

Luca was the only addition to our team, and we had to hope we were enough. Ashley had barely been able to open her eyes when I checked on her, and we'd left her to sleep.

We could have used her as muscle, but we would have to do without. There were five of us, four with magical or supernatural defences. I was the only one without.

I didn't have more mundane weapons either, not even a can of pepper spray. My plan was to hide behind the others if it came to a confrontation. Maybe yell threateningly and shake my fist in the air.

The sky was overcast, and it was dark by the time we reached the same street outside the cemetery on which

Saved by the Spell

Amber had parked the car before. We were dressed in all black; even Kane was wearing black jeans and a black cashmere jumper instead of a suit, which ... I approved.

If he was annoyed with me for ruining his suit, he didn't bring it up.

"Spooky," Luca noted as we waited in darkness for Kane to open the bicycle lock holding the side gate closed.

"Shouldn't you love cemeteries?" I teased him to hide my nervousness. The cemetery had been beautiful and eerie during the day, but at night it suddenly seemed frightening.

He shot me a sideways look. "Why would I love them? There's nothing to eat there."

I shuddered and he grinned. I'd been too chicken to ask if he truly drank blood—he ate perfectly normal food too—so I had no idea if he was messing with me or not.

I wasn't sure I wanted to find out. The whole supernatural world was a learning curve for me, and I was determined to take it slow.

We took the straightest path to the Terrace Catacombs, which is to say, wandered around the cemetery trying to reach there as directly as possible.

There were no lamps illuminating the paths, and with the foliage arcing over the paths, blocking the ambient light from the neighbourhood, I could barely see where I was going—a problem that didn't seem to affect the rest. I knew Luca had excellent night vision, but the others must have opted for a spell.

Pity no one came to think of mundane old me. But I didn't dare to take out my phone and use its light, in case it messed with the night vision of the rest of them.

I stumbled once more, and Luca offered me an arm. I hesitated only briefly before accepting it; it was either that or fall on my face.

"Doesn't it make you feel sick to hold me?"

He shrugged, which I more felt against my side than saw. "I'm getting used to it. Besides, we'll never get there if you break your leg."

Practical.

The moon, three quarters full, appeared from behind the clouds. I still couldn't see where I was going, but it hit the marble angels that sprang from here and there from the darkness. What had seemed charming during the day turned downright frightening in the moonlight.

"This is not the best time to remember the weeping angels from *Doctor Who*…" Luca muttered.

We glanced at each other and leaned closer. Spell or no spell, I wasn't so repulsive he wouldn't use me as protection against angel statues creeping on us.

I was twelve when I saw that episode and I'd had nightmares for months. My parents forbade me from watching *Doctor Who* because of it, but of course I watched it in secret. But the series never again came as close to frightening me as that episode had.

"They are imaginary, right?" I had to ask. If werewolves and vampires were real, maybe those statues were too.

He shrugged, which didn't help.

I took his hand, and he didn't shake it away.

"So … is the Highgate Vampire real, then?" I had to ask, as if I weren't spooked enough as it was.

The Highgate Vampire had been some sort of media sensation in the seventies, presumably living in or

Saved by the Spell

haunting the cemetery. It was long before I was born, but if Luca was as old as he claimed, he might know.

He snorted. "No. And I know. I went to look."

"Are there many of your kind around?" I asked, suddenly curious.

"Nope."

There was finality in his tone that didn't invite to asking more, so I let the matter be.

Finally, we reached the Terrace Catacombs, with me still in one piece, thanks to Luca's firm hand and fast reflexes. Standing at the top of the hill, not shadowed by trees, the limestone wall shone eerily in the moonlight. But the door to the Stanford crypt somehow managed to be deep in shadows.

"I hope that doesn't mean the warlock wards are back," I muttered to Luca. We waited for Kane to study the door, standing far enough that if he was catapulted by the wards again, he wouldn't fall on us.

Chivalrous of us, I know.

Kane made a gesture with his hand and the wards protecting the crypt suddenly lit up the night. I'd never seen anything like it.

I glanced around. "Those had better come down soon. We're visible miles away."

"How are you supposed to get through those?" Luca asked, amazed.

The wards covered the front of the crypt from ground to the roof, twirling around and through each other in colourful swirls, making it impossible to see where they began or ended. I didn't know anything about magic, but that had to be an overkill of protection.

And this was without the black magic wards. They probably wouldn't have been so cheerful looking.

"That's why you're all here," Kane said, not taking his eyes off the wards. "If Phoebe could stand next to Amber...?"

Amber and Giselle had already taken their places on both sides of him, and I did as I was asked.

"And Luca, you'll stand next to Giselle. Good. Now, Phoebe, place your hand on that green line above Amber's orange line, and Luca, you put your right hand on the same green line on this end, and left hand on that blue one below."

I placed my hand on the instructed spot. The wall hummed under my hand, tingling, but it didn't try to throw me back or repel me. Kane nodded.

"Now, Phoebe, when I give you a sign, you'll have to place your other hand on that pink spot at the upper edge."

I located it and nodded. I could reach it.

Kane began to chant with a steady voice, which I hadn't witnessed him do with wards before, and Giselle and Amber joined him. With every syllable, I felt power rising. The wall of wards under my hand started to hum, resonating with the chanting. Tingling spread up my arm and down my entire body until my feet were buzzing. It wasn't painful, but it made me want to squirm.

I didn't dare to complain or fidget though. The wall had to come down.

The voices grew louder and the power intensified. Just as I thought I wouldn't be able to handle it any longer, Kane bellowed, "Now!" and I hit my palm on the pink ward.

A jolt of energy shot through me. My muscles contracted and I bit my tongue when my jaw suddenly

Saved by the Spell

locked, drawing blood. If I could've moved, I would've yanked my hands off the wards.

The wards came down so fast we all fell forward, dropping on our hands and knees. I leaned my palms on the cool grass, panting heavily. Everyone was doing the same.

I would have been content to stay there till morning, but Kane pushed onto his feet, brushing off his jeans. "Shall we continue?"

He helped Giselle and Luca up, and Amber and I rose by leaning on each other. My legs were tottery, but I could walk. My scalp was buzzing, and I was sure my hair had shot up like I'd been hit by lightning.

Kane looked mostly put-together, but his hair was billowing more than usual. Gingerly, he reached for the door handle. We held our breaths, but it didn't repel him, and he pulled.

Despite the obvious age of the iron plate door, it opened easily and silently, as if it had been greased. Kane didn't step in though, having learned his lesson, but checked the doorway for wards and traps. When he deemed the doorway safe, he conjured a ball of light and sent it into the crypt, revealing a small space of maybe four metres by four.

An *empty* small space.

Eighteen

WE FILED IN, FILLING THE PLACE, and looked around in dismay. It smelled of earth and damp stone, and nothing else. I was glad there were no remains of whomever the crypt belonged to, but it should have had something. It didn't even have a sarcophagus, let alone those pigeonholes for coffins like inside the gallery.

"I can't believe Blackhart would've erected such vicious wards if Rupert wasn't here," Amber huffed, disappointed.

"He must be here," Kane stated, fists pressed on his hips, as if he were stubbornly refusing to believe his eyes. But we didn't have to rely on them alone.

"Do you still have Rupert's pen you spelled to track him?"

Perking, he fished it out from his pocket. He held it on his palm, and turned a circle. "According to this, Rupert is here. The wards blocked the signal completely before."

"It must give you a wrong signal now, because clearly he's not here," Giselle said. "How about Jack?"

Kane shook his head. "My spell doesn't sense him."

"Maybe he left while we were away," she suggested.

"I couldn't sense him even when we presumed he was still at the cemetery."

"The wards blocked him too," Amber noted.

"And we did come here assuming that there are tunnels from here deep enough to block your spell," I pointed out, and Luca perked.

"There has to be a hidden door in the walls or the floor. Let's look for a trigger."

We each took one wall and Kane the floor, stomping on the large sandstones. My wall—or indeed any of them—didn't have any discerning features, reliefs, or handy wall scones to push or pull. Just plane stones.

Considering there was another crypt on the other side of my wall, I wasn't expecting miracles, but I pressed every stone I could reach. They didn't budge. The others weren't successful either. But no one was willing to give up. We'd worked too hard to get through the wards. And we had to find Rupert.

"Sherlock Holmes would spot handy scrapes on the floor where the secret door opened," I muttered, frustrated. "But there are none here."

Kane cocked his head sideways, his eyes sharpening as he considered my words. Then he straightened as if he'd figured out something important. He stood in front of the back wall and began to make gestures with his arms, hands, and fingers, bending them, locking them together and opening again, in complicated sequences. Then he slapped his palms together.

The back wall of the crypt disappeared as if it had never been there.

Saved by the Spell

Behind the false wall, two more metres of room was revealed. We stared at it with our mouths open.

Kane looked satisfied, Amber dismayed. "It felt like a perfectly real wall to me," she said, "and I went over every inch. Blackhart must be more powerful than we thought to be able to create such a convincing illusion."

Not a happy thought.

The false wall had hidden a large limestone sarcophagus placed sideways against the real back wall like an altar. Kane rushed to it, as if pulled by the pen.

"Quick. Rupert is in here." He checked it for wards and then tried to lift the lid, but it wouldn't budge.

"There could be a lever for moving it," I suggested, but nothing immediately looked like one.

"I'll open it," Luca declared, and Kane stepped aside.

Luca took a position at the head of the sarcophagus, placed the heels of his palms under the lid like a weightlifter, and pushed up, his muscles bulging with supernatural strength. The lid rose with deceptive ease, and he glided it to the side, the stone grinding against stone with a horrible sound that made my teeth ache.

When it had opened enough, we leaned gingerly over to peek in. Rupert was lying on his back at the bottom, arms crossed over his chest. He glowered at us.

"What kept you?"

~ ~ ~

RUPERT'S LEGS WERE TOTTERY when we finally managed to fish him out—and that was with magical assistance. But considering he was close to a hundred and had been held in a cold limestone sarcophagus for twenty-four hours in his smoking jacket, flannel trousers, and slippers, he was doing amazingly well. Soon he could stand without support.

Perhaps the same magic that kept him spritely despite his age had helped him through his ordeal too.

"Let's get you to a doctor for a check-up," Giselle said worriedly, about to lead him out of the crypt. But he pulled away, refusing to be moved.

"I'm not going anywhere until that dastardly fiend has been found!"

He was full of fire for someone who should be dead or at least feebly heading to a hospital, preferably in an ambulance. His amber hair was billowing with anger like Kane's.

"You are more important than Blackhart," Kane said, but Rupert shot him an imperious look.

"If we don't stop him, my importance doesn't matter."

If it had been up to me, I'd have considered taking him away against his will. He was ancient and we outnumbered him. How difficult could it be? But the others were more law abiding, or knew him better, and they gave in.

"Exactly where do you think we'll start looking for him?" Amber asked, crossing her arms over her chest.

Rupert patted the sarcophagus. "Here."

Kane leaned closer. "They go through the sarcophagus?"

"No, they go under it. The whole thing moves. I felt it when I was inside."

"Fascinating..." Kane rounded to the other side of the sturdy structure and began pushing the reliefs on it.

Saved by the Spell

I really hoped there was a mechanical trigger. It had taken Luca's vampire strength to move just the lid. It would be impossible to move the whole thing.

"There are grooves here where it's moved towards the back wall." Luca pointed at the curving scrapes on the floor. "I'd say it's this end that moves."

He moved to the opposite side from the grooves, leaned his shoulder against the stone like in a rugby scrum, and began to push.

At first, nothing happened. Then he must have triggered the opening mechanism because the sarcophagus suddenly disappeared from under him. The heavy edifice glided aside so easily and fast it pushed him off balance, almost plunging him headfirst down the stairs that were revealed under it.

He grinned, steadying himself on the sarcophagus. "Easy."

We stared at the stairs. They were shallow redbrick steps that went down so far that the light of Kane's magical ball didn't reach the bottom.

"These are old steps," Kane noted. Each step was worn in the middle, indicating that they had been used a lot at some point in their past.

I couldn't understand why they were there. "Do you think the Sanfords built them?"

He scratched his neck, intrigued. "I'd say they're older than the cemetery. Let's see where they lead."

He went down first, dipping his head as he dove under the sarcophagus, but the ceiling rose soon after and he could walk straight, although the vaulting brick ceiling almost brushed the top of his head.

The rest of us followed. Some of us—me—more reluctantly than the others.

I was the last to enter, and I leaned my side heavily against the wall, more out of fear than for support. I needed the solid feel of the bricks to ground me. It would turn my clothes red with brick dust, but I didn't care.

I'd taken only a couple of steps down when I felt a brick give in under my shoulder, and there was an audible click. I pulled hastily back, but it was too late.

Above my head, as fast as it had opened, the sarcophagus glided back to its former position, closing us in. The last click echoed in the stairway. The silence after it was deafening, pressing my bones.

"I'm sorry," I said miserably. I wasn't claustrophobic, but this seemed like the perfect place and time to develop it. I had to steel my knees not to slump on the stairs.

"We'll be able to open it again," Kane consoled me.

"And likely there is a way out at the other end," Rupert said. "I never detected them coming back once they'd gone in."

It didn't stop me from feeling wretched.

"Do you want to hold my hand?" Lucas asked.

I ignored his teasing smile and nodded. "I'll let you know."

It might yet come to that.

I gestured for them to proceed, taking the rear. The stairwell was only wide enough for one person at a time, and it would be a tight fit if we wanted to switch places.

The steps went down for a good while, before levelling up into a tunnel. The walls and floor were brick, there were no cave-ins, and everything was dry, indicating that whoever had built it knew what they were doing.

I asked aloud what all of us had to be wondering: "Where do you think this leads to?"

Saved by the Spell

"If I were to hazard a guess, to the erstwhile cellar of the manor that once stood here," Rupert said with an authoritative tone that stated he was certain of it. "I think the tunnel was made by the family who owned it, maybe centuries ago."

"Why would they need such a tunnel?"

He shrugged. He wasn't at all winded by our walk, and his back was almost as straight as Kane's, the slight stoop of his shoulders caused by a century of bending over books rather than age.

"Maybe they were Catholic. Catholicism was only made legal around the time the manor was taken down. Many Catholic houses had old escape tunnels and priest's holes."

I nodded, as I knew it. But abstract knowledge was different than witnessing the reality of it.

"Or maybe they were a mage family," he then added.

Everyone looked grim. Apparently, mages had been living in fear for their lives too, even though most people didn't even know they existed.

Rupert was right. Not long after, we emerged from the tunnel into a vaulted cellar. Like the tunnel, it was in general good repair despite its obvious age, the ceiling holding and the support columns still sturdy. Brick steps led up at the other end.

Only, there was no door at the top.

Bricks blocked the space where it had been, old but different from the walls, indicating that the doorway or hatch out had been sealed when the manor was taken down. There was probably a ton of earth above it.

A sheen of sweat broke out on my skin at the thought. I looked frantically around, trying to locate a way out, but there were no doors, nothing to indicate that people were able to leave the space.

"What the hell?" I exclaimed.

"There could be another hidden door," Luca suggested, but unlike in the crypt, no grooves marred the uneven redbrick floor to handily reveal where it might be.

There had been plenty of traffic in the room too, but though the floor was dusty there were no clear traces revealing the direction they had gone.

"If this is Blackhart's lair, it leaves a lot to wish for," I huffed.

Amber tilted her head, studying the place with an intense look. "But he must have a reason for coming here."

"Maybe he comes here to cast illegal spells undetected," Kane suggested. "Some of them could leave a trace that other mages can spot."

I imagined Blackhart performing a sacrifice here, to become a warlock. The cemetery was a handy place to hide a body too. I glanced around, but there were no chalk lines on the floor—or blood for that matter.

I shuddered.

"Are all these walls real?" Giselle asked, patting the one closest to her.

"Let's see," Kane said. With Rupert observing him like the old, strict, teacher he undoubtedly was, Kane cast the same spell as in the crypt. Nothing happened. Each wall remained where they were.

I was starting to seriously dislike this place.

Rupert was the only one not ruffled by the situation. At his age, he'd probably seen everything many times and didn't have a ruffle to give anymore.

Saved by the Spell

He walked slowly around the small space, feeling the air with his hand, occasionally wiggling his finger so minutely I couldn't be sure if it was magic-related.

Eventually, he settled in the middle of the floor and spread his arms wide to his sides. He held them easily up, and they weren't shaking at all. "Please, step behind me."

We hurried to comply, not wanting to be caught up in whatever spell he was about to perform.

He concentrated, and before our eyes transformed from an old man to an archmage to be reckoned with. His stooping shoulders straightened, and his pose became powerful. Magical energy filled him, making his hair billow. I could have sworn he was glowing lightly.

He squeezed his hands into fists, and I felt the power build. Again, it was different from Kane's, but unlike Dufort's it didn't irritate my skin. It felt like plunging into a slightly too hot bath; shocking initially, but ultimately good for you.

When the power had risen enough, Rupert banged his fists together in front of his chest. A sudden vacuum made my ears pop as the magic drained from the room.

A portal opened. It was dark on the other side, but there was definitely a room there.

"How did you do that?" Kane demanded, angry and a little suspicious.

Rupert shot him an annoyed glance. "Relax, boy. I didn't create the portal. I simply triggered the permanent spell that opens it for those who don't know how to create them."

"Jack," I said.

"And whoever else is in league with Blackhart. There were several people going in through the crypt, but always one at the time, so I didn't have a chance to detect their voices."

"Why didn't you ask one of them to help you out?" Giselle demanded. "They can't all be so far lost that they wouldn't have helped you."

Rupert glared at her from under his bushy brows. "Do you take me for an old fool? Of course I tried, but the inside of the sarcophagus was spelled, and I couldn't spare energy for breaking it, as I had no idea how long it would take for you to find me. I yelled at you too, but you didn't hear me, did you?"

Giselle shook her head, a little sheepishly.

"Now, let's step through before it collapses," Rupert ordered, going in first, before Kane could stop him.

He and Luca hurried to follow, with Giselle and Amber right at their heels. I was at the back of the group, so I was last to approach the portal.

The moment the mages were through, the light balls they'd conjured abruptly died, plunging the cellar into darkness. Only the light glow of the portal itself offered some illumination.

I hurried to catch them, but in the darkness I couldn't see where I was stepping. One of the uneven bricks tripped me, and I almost fell.

Stumbling forward, I made to plunge through the portal headfirst, when it suddenly died. Unable to stop my motion, I fell on the floor. The pain of the bricks grounding to my hands and knees barely registered from my shock.

I was left in the pitch-black cellar. Alone.

Trapped.

Nineteen

DESPERATION WASHED OVER ME, turning my bones into liquid. I leaned heavily against my hands, fighting to keep the contents of my stomach in.

I was trapped. I would die in an underground cellar no one even knew existed. The air felt heavy, as if the ceiling were lowering, pressing me, robbing me of air. I imagined the ton of earth above collapsing, all the scarier because I couldn't see it happening—or not happening.

Panic swallowed me. I'd never been so frightened in my life. My breathing came in shallow gasps that only managed to make me dizzy.

I don't know how long I just sat there leaning on my hands, panting. Little by little, my heart slowed down, and my breathing turned easier, mostly because I'd run out of reasons to panic. The ceiling obligingly stayed where it should.

I made sure of it by reaching up as high as I could with my hand.

With oxygen reintroduced to my brain, reason returned. My friends knew where I was. They would come for me.

That they weren't here yet had to mean that they couldn't open the portal on the other side. They'd have to return to the cemetery with more mundane transportation. It might take an hour or two. I could handle it.

Maybe.

Then a more worrisome thought hit. The portal might have opened on the other side of the world—or Outer Hebrides, which amounted for the same as far as my chances for a speedy rescue went. It might take them days to return to the crypt.

And what if they couldn't come for me at all? What if the portal led to Blackhart's lair and he'd been waiting for them? They could have been captured.

That sent me down another spiral of panic.

Gritting my teeth, I fought to a semblance of calm. I wasn't trapped. And I didn't need my friends to rescue me. There was a trigger on this side of the sarcophagus. The crypt belonged to ordinary humans who didn't know portals existed; they needed a way out of this cellar.

What I needed to do was to return to the sarcophagus and find the trigger.

I had to get to the tunnel.

I glanced around in the dark, as if I'd be able to spot the mouth of the tunnel, but the blackness was absolute. The way out could be anywhere. I'd lost what little awareness I'd had of the room already before I lost the light.

Unwilling to stand, fearing I'd trip again, I headed in a random direction on all fours. The edges of the uneven

Saved by the Spell

bricks ground into my knees, but I went doggedly on until I hit the wall.

Literally. I banged my head on it with startling force.

Rubbing my forehead, I slumped against the sturdy bricks. There had to be an easier way to find the tunnel than crawling around the room.

And there was.

My mobile phone! I don't know why I hadn't come to think of it before.

With shaking hands, I dug it out of my pocket. There was no reception—big surprise—but it had a light app.

Carefully, fearing I'd drop the damn thing and break it, I hit the torch icon and light poured out. I blinked, trying to adjust my eyes.

And maybe stem the tears of relief too that blurred my vision.

With light, I finally felt secure. Or at least less frightened. But I couldn't dawdle in case the battery died.

Forcing myself to stand, I swept the cellar with the light and found the tunnel opposite to where I was. With the light illuminating my way, I crossed the floor, careful not to trip again. But once I was in the tunnel, I hurried on, no matter how I tried to make myself walk carefully.

The tunnel seemed shorter this time round, but I wasn't complaining. Soon, I was at the foot of the steps, and I hurried up, unable to care for safety anymore. I needed to get out of here.

I was panting when I reached the top, more out of newly rising panic than exhaustion—or maybe claustrophobia was finally kicking in.

I didn't give myself time to rest and began to push the bricks on the wall where I'd triggered the opening before.

I didn't immediately discover it and I feared I'd imagined doing it. Maybe the sarcophagus had closed on its own?

Then my hand hit the right one and the limestone tomb began to move aside. Fresh air poured in and I drew in deep gulps, barely waiting for the gap to be large enough for me to fit through before climbing out.

I dropped on my knees for sheer relief and sat there leaning on my hands again, until I felt sufficiently strong enough to push to my feet.

A scrape of a foot on the crypt floor made all the hairs in my body shoot up in fear. I wasn't alone.

The pressure in my neck returned with a vengeance too, as if it wanted to burn a hole through my skin. Was Jack here?

Before I managed to point the phone's light into the crypt, a magical light ball flared to life, illuminating the space. And in the middle stood the mage who had conjured it.

Only it was no one I had imagined.

~ ~ ~

"Why…? How…?"

I couldn't form a coherent sentence. My mind was blank as I studied the woman standing in front of me, tall and confident in her jeans and high-heeled boots, only a sheer black blouse covering her against the chillness of the night and the perpetually cool crypt.

"What are you doing here?"

Ida sneered. All the laughter I'd associated with her was gone. It was as if she'd removed a mask to reveal a stranger.

"I'm here to take you captive."

Saved by the Spell

I blinked, trying to wrap my mind around her words. "Why?"

I simply couldn't fathom why she was here—doing magic. How could she be a mage and not tell me? I'd told her about the spell—in jest, but still. She could have told me she was a mage then.

She gave me a slow look. "You released Rupert and I need leverage."

"For what?"

"For challenging Kane."

"You? But you're not..." *even a mage*. But I wisely left that out because of course she was. She was here, conjuring a magical light ball. "...part of their council," I finished feebly instead. Kane would have recognised her if she was.

I switched off the light app, as it was useless now, and slipped the phone into my back pocket. Ida folded her arms across her chest.

"That's not actually a requirement. I belong to the council of my hometown."

"I thought you were from London." Though in truth, we'd never talked about it. I'd merely assumed because she lived here. "My friends said there are no Sanfords who are mages."

"Why would you think I inherited it from my *father*?" Her lip curled in distaste with the last word, giving me a notion that she didn't hold him in much esteem.

I hadn't imagined her inheriting it anywhere, but I shrugged, and she leaned forward, launching into a lecture.

"Magic tends to be matrilinear. Grimshaws, my mother's family, are well known and respected mages in York, where I've lived ever since she divorced my father when I was six. And after she married Julius's father when I was eleven, we became even more influential."

Julius? I shook my head, trying to connect the name. "You mean ... *Blackhart*?"

I could barely say it aloud, I was so badly shocked.

"Of course I do," she huffed, as if I were an idiot.

Which ... fair enough. In my wildest imaginations, I hadn't pictured her stepbrother to be Julius Blackhart. She'd talked about bringing him to our cousins' wedding as her date, for heaven's sake.

So what did it mean, knowing that the two of them were together?

"York is no longer enough for you?" Then I remembered why Blackhart was here. "Are you helping him to take over London?"

"No!" she spat. "And I didn't think you'd be so sexist that you'd reduce a woman to a mere assistant."

The contempt on her face was clear. I thought it best not to point out that my assessment sprang from the notion that Blackhart was the more powerful mage—and that no one had talked about her with such fear, or at all. She would probably have taken that the wrong way too, and I couldn't antagonise her more than I had, if I wanted to survive this.

"*I* will take over the London council and Julius will replace Rupert as the archmage. We'll rule London together. And from here..." She spread her arms as if encompassing the whole world. "...who knows."

It was a solid plan as far as crazy power grabs went. I nodded, as if I approved.

"So what do you need me for? Just challenge Kane already." Then it hit me: "You can't. You're not powerful

Saved by the Spell

enough to take him in a fair challenge. You need him to concede."

I sneered. A big mistake.

Her eyes flashed in anger, and with a flick of her hand she had me immobilised. I could barely move my head, but at least my mouth worked.

"I'm seriously starting to hate this spell."

"Shut up, or I'll close your mouth with it too," she growled.

That silenced me—for a heartbeat. "So are you going to keep me here? I mean, you're a fit lass, but I seriously doubt you can carry me." The spell rendered the body rigidly immobile. It would be like moving a log or a statue.

She made a couple of movements with her hands, and I found myself being tipped on my back so fast that my stomach lurched and so carelessly that I hit my head on the edge of the sarcophagus behind me.

Lights sparkled in my eyes for the pain. I must've blacked out briefly too, because the next thing I knew, we were travelling down the tunnel I'd just exited.

I had not wanted to be back here.

I was hovering on my back, not high up, because my braid was brushing the tunnel floor. Apparently it wasn't subject to the binding spell. It tugged my scalp as it snagged the uneven bricks.

Ida walked ahead of me, pulling me behind her on an invisible leash. My body bumped on the tunnel walls constantly, but she didn't care.

At least it wasn't my head again.

"So how does Jack fit in all this?"

She yanked the leash and I banged against the wall with force. That would leave a bruise.

"Why are you talking again?"

"Because I'm morbidly curious?"

We reached the cellar, and she released the hovering spell. I dropped to the floor with a thud that emptied my lungs. I hit my head again too, but at least I didn't lose consciousness this time.

I should have worn my hair in a bun. It would have softened the blow.

"Jack is a useful tool."

On that, I agreed with her.

"It didn't look like that when you kissed outside his home this afternoon."

Her face appeared above me, upside down as she leaned to stare down at me with a derisive smirk. "Did it not occur to you that I staged it for your benefit?"

It absolutely had not.

"How would you even have known I was there?"

We'd been well hidden, I was sure of it.

"I put a tracking spell on you," she said smugly, startling me so badly that I tried to sit up, forgetting that the spell kept me immobile.

"You?" I owed Jack an apology for thinking it had been him. "You must not be very good at it, because I felt you."

She snorted. "That was just an addition to the spell I've invented. It allows me to poke you whenever I want."

"Why would you want to do that?" I asked, hurt.

"To mess with you. Do you know how much fun I've had in the Tube, watching you twirl around trying to locate the source and never even spot me?"

That was a rotten thing to do.

"But you didn't even know me before the engagement party. Why would you want to be mean to me?" I sounded like a little girl, but I was truly upset.

Saved by the Spell

"Who says I don't know you? Julius and I have been planning this for months already. Years. We've kept an eye on all the important players in London and no one is more important than Kane, and through him, you. I know everything about you."

And here I'd thought Danielle had been spying on me, but now that I came to think of it, it wouldn't suit her at all. She was a warlock in making. She didn't do stakeouts. She would delegate.

"So your brother saved the good jobs like taking over the world for Danielle, and you were given the shitty ones?"

Her hand squeezed into a fist, and I was sure she would punch me. There was nothing I could do to block it. But she gained control of her anger.

"My brother foolishly became enamoured with her, but he saw his error. Now he's placing his trust in me."

"Yet you're here doing the humdrum job again, whereas Jack…" I pretended to look around, even though my head didn't really move.

"Where is he anyway?"

"Why? Do you hope he'll come and save you?" She huffed, amused. "You do realise that he's the one who put the spell on you that makes you repulsive to men? And he wouldn't have known how to cast it without my help."

My brows shot up as a piece of a puzzle became clear. "So it was you who helped him to break into the library."

I guess I owed Danielle an apology too.

Nah.

"Yes. So you know he's not good enough to best me. He couldn't rescue you even if he wanted, which he doesn't."

"You never know, he might," I taunted her, even though I hadn't even considered it. I'd rather rot in here than accept his help. "After all, he's not repulsed by me. Why is that, anyway?"

She shrugged, but her need to lecture won. "Turned out, it's built into the spell, which we only learned at the engagement party." Her eyes flashed. She had not been as happy about it as she had let on. Maybe she had intended for him to be repulsed by me too, only he had started flirting with me instead.

"Whoever casts it is immune. Fathers needed to be able to be around their bespelled daughters. But mostly medieval husbands used it to keep their wives faithful while they were fighting in the Crusades and other wars. They'd be gone for years and could be sure that she hadn't been with any other man in the meanwhile."

"But surely he'd just break the spell when he came home?"

She laughed, and it sounded horrible. "You're assuming it can be broken. How funny."

My stomach turned cold, and I had to swallow hard to keep the bile down. I couldn't turn my head far enough to throw up. I'd choke in my own vomit if I wasn't careful.

"We have the spell book you used," I managed to say, but my voice had lost its earlier strength. She could not be right. I couldn't be repulsive for the rest of my life.

"The book doesn't contain the counter-spell. If it ever existed, it's long lost."

Desperation began to creep in, but I couldn't give into it. "Rupert will figure out something."

She made a dismissive gesture with her hand. "Provided he'll survive. In fact, I'm not entirely sure the

Saved by the Spell

spell is something you'll need to worry much longer either."

I did not like the sound of that.

She turned her back to me and stood in the middle of the floor, like Rupert had earlier. I couldn't feel her gathering the magical energy, but she likely knew the quick way to open the portal.

I had no idea where she would be taking me, but it couldn't be anywhere I wanted to be.

"What was the point of making me repulsive to men anyway?" I asked to stall her.

She glanced at me over her shoulder. "To unsettle Kane, of course."

I rolled my eyes, the only part of my body I had some control over, apart from my mouth—and we can probably agree I wasn't wholly in control of that.

"You guys have to stop believing that he's into me. Danielle made that mistake and look where it got her."

Back to the arms of her hot lover, but I'd best not to mention that.

Ida abandoned her spell and moved to my side to look at me the right way up. She leaned closer and I contemplated spitting at her face, but that wouldn't have accomplished anything.

"It doesn't matter whether he is romantically interested in you or not. It's straining for him to be around you. He has to use magical energy to shield from the effects, and it drains him. It'll make it easy for me to take him down."

I cocked a brow, challenging, as if I were in a position to do so. "He hasn't shown any signs of weakness so far. He bested Jack in no time yesterday."

She pulled straight. "What?"

I found her reaction interesting. "You didn't know? Jack challenged Kane. He lost, of course."

"He wouldn't dare," she practically growled.

I made to shrug, even though my shoulders wouldn't move. "He would if Blackhart ordered him."

I'd never even met the man, but the way Danielle and Jack feared him, I thought it was a fair assumption.

"I'll fucking end him."

Oops.

Twenty

IDA OPENED THE PORTAL WITH AN angry flicker of her hand, and the next thing I knew, she yanked me through it after her. My feet were barely on the other side when the portal closed.

With her light ball illuminating the way, I tried to look around as she pulled me out of the room we'd arrived in, but I mostly saw the ceiling. Based on its neoclassical motifs, I presumed it was from the 18th century. The walls looked like they were papered during a later era though. But what did I know? I was only a humble antiques dealer—or his assistant.

The furniture I managed to spy from my position near the floor definitely roused my professional interest.

"Ooh, is that a Louis XVI commode? Can we stop? We have a client looking for one."

But she yanked me so sharply by the invisible leash that my head hit the back of her knee and she fell on her stomach with an *oomph*.

I barely managed to swallow my snicker.

Fine, I laughed.

She pushed herself back on her feet and continued without a word. We were in a hallway that had portraits—mediocre, probably by country painters—on one side, and deep window embrasures on the other. It was a long hallway, with doors to hidden rooms at intervals, and with runners covering the floor—I presumed by the soft thuds her heels made against it.

At the other end, there was a grand staircase, which we took down one floor. I glided down headfirst, with her slowing my descent via her invisible leash.

I guess I should be grateful she didn't just let go of it and let my weight carry me down.

She entered the first room on the right. I found myself in a large space with a high ceiling that had chubby cherubs painted on it, lots of windows on one side, and magnificent chandeliers with oak leaf crystals offering brilliant light. The floor had to be hardwood, because Ida's heels made a staccato sound against it as she dragged me deeper.

"Is this a ballroom?"

She paused in the middle. "No, this is where my brother casts his spells."

"In a ballroom? With cherubs?"

This was not at all what I'd imagined. This was an elegant space from an elegant era, not the lair of an evil mage.

"Where are we anyway?"

"In the Blackhart manor in York," she said, taking a great deal of pleasure as she announced how far from London we were. It wasn't quite the remote part of Scottish islands I'd imagined, but it wasn't exactly within the M25 either that circled Greater London.

"York?"

Saved by the Spell

Was this where my friends had come to as well? If so, where were they now?

"Why here?"

She shrugged. "He owns the place. The portal allows him to travel to London as fast as he pleases."

"So why is the other end hidden under the cemetery?"

"Why are you asking all these questions?" she demanded, leaning over me again.

I looked her straight in the eyes. "I thought we already established I'm curious. And you like to lecture."

She gave me a fed-up look, but proceeded to answer as she straightened: "It takes a great deal of energy to maintain a permanent portal like that one. Not only would other mages be able to detect it, the cemetery is actually a good source for the energy."

"What, the bodies?"

"Yes."

"But ... they're centuries old."

"The older the better for generating the kind of energy needed for it."

I shuddered in disgust.

"So Blackhart is a warlock, then?"

"No."

My brows shot up at her denial. "But only they can create a portal."

She huffed. "Did Kane tell you that? Perhaps Rupert isn't as powerful as he pretends to be if he hasn't taught his successor how to do it. Ellis was definitely able to tell Julius how it's done."

Kane wasn't Rupert's apprentice, but I wouldn't give her that piece of information. Not for free, anyway.

"Am I supposed to believe that using corpses to juice up the portal is benign magic?"

217

Instead of answering, she released the spell keeping me hovering and I dropped to the floor again. That it was hardwood instead of brick didn't make my landing any softer. Tears of pain smarted my eyes, but I blinked them away.

"So what happens now?" I asked once I could speak without showing my pain and fear.

"Now I prepare you for Blackhart."

That sounded ominous.

"To have a nice candlelight supper with him?" I suggested hopefully, but she wasn't amused.

"You will be the key to his ascension."

"Into what?" But I already knew. "Warlock."

I almost lost control of my bladder, which I was amazed to realise hadn't happened yet.

"Why does he need to become a warlock? I thought he had a superior archmage teaching him."

She walked to the other end of the room, her heels clicking. There was a scraping sound like something heavy was being dragged down the floor and I winced.

"That'll ruin the floor!"

"Can't be helped," she panted. It took me a moment to figure out why she wasn't using the levitation spell, and then I sneered.

"You don't have strength to use the levitation spell anymore. Why you presume you can beat Kane in a battle of magic, I have no idea."

She huffed—or grunted in effort more like. "First up, if you think I'd be able to move this thing without magic, you're delusional. Secondly, I don't have to challenge him. He'll abdicate to save your life."

I hated how relieved I felt hearing it. "I'm not to die?"

Saved by the Spell

"Oh, you'll die. But only after Kane has made me the leader of the London council."

Great.

She pushed a large wall made of marble next to me. Next thing I knew, the ceiling seemed to come closer, and I experienced a brief disorientation. It took me a moment to realise she was lifting me up with the levitation spell again. She lowered me onto what felt like cold stone, slightly more gently this time. Was it marble too? Was I on an altar of some kind? One fit for a human sacrifice, no doubt.

I shuddered in fear—and my foot twitched.

I held my breath, fearing I'd imagined it. Slowly, carefully, so as not to draw Ida's attention, I tried to curl my fingers. Left side moved, but the right side didn't—yet. It was my dominant hand, and I needed it.

I tried to lift my head too, but my braid was stuck under me, and it stopped the movement as effectively as the binding spell.

I really should have worn my hair in a bun.

Ida's face appeared above me, much closer now that I'd been lifted onto the altar. I stilled, fearing she'd noticed my wiggling. Was she losing control of the spell? Was there any way I could speed up the process?

"It's a pity we have to use you for this," she said, sounding genuinely regretful. "We would've had so much fun at our cousins' wedding."

Was she for real? Then again, without all this nonsense, we probably would have had fun. I'd liked her.

"The wedding's called off, remember? Jack ruined it."

Her features tightened with anger. "And he'll pay for that."

I considered suggesting she swap me for him as a sacrifice, but I wasn't so far gone yet.

"It's only a wedding. They'll find someone else."

She looked at me like I was an idiot. "Do you have any idea how long it took me to find Olivia for Henry?"

My mouth dropped. "What do you mean?"

"I was the one who introduced Olivia to him. I made sure they fell in love. Though even I didn't anticipate they'd move so fast." Her smile was smug.

"Kane said one can't make people fall in love with magic." It wasn't exactly a useful comment, but I was too stunned to say anything sensible.

"You don't need magic to manipulate two people into thinking they're madly in love."

"You don't?" Now there was a skill she could build a business on and rule the world without magic. "But why would you do that?"

She placed a hand on her chest, looking exalted. "Julius and I are determined to elevate mages to where we belong. And for that we need more mages. That means more mage marriages for mage babies."

"But Henry isn't a mage. Not even from a mage family." She'd said so herself.

"But Olivia is."

She could have dropped me with a feather. "She's what? A mage?"

"Of mage lineage." She looked self-important. "I went through centuries of family lines of magicians to find a suitable bride for Henry, and I found her."

Was that searing sensation inside me jealousy? Or envy, more like? I hadn't realised I wanted to be a mage so badly, but knowing Olivia could be and I wasn't really stung.

Saved by the Spell

"There are mages in her father's family?"

She shook her head. "No, her mother's. Your great-aunt Beverly was a mage."

~ ~ ~

I STARED AT HER FOR A FEW stunned heartbeats. Then I snorted such a throaty laugh that I almost choked. "That's brilliant. Until now, I thought you were at least remotely sane, but you're completely mental, aren't you?"

She slapped me. Hard. I tasted blood where the inside of my cheek rubbed my teeth.

But as much as it hurt, I took solace in noticing that my head had moved from the force of it.

Her magical binding on me was slipping again.

"My grandmother's sister was not a mage," I stated with surety, though in truth I didn't remember her well. She died when I was six, but she'd seemed perfectly normal to my child's eye.

"Do not doubt me," she said, her tone threatening.

"You seriously expect me to believe that you have a breeding programme planned based on the remote possibility that a random person would carry the gene to her offspring? And why Olivia and not me? Great-Aunt Beverly was my family too."

"I told you. It goes down in matrilinear lines. You're related to Beverly through your father, so you're not as strong a candidate. Beverly didn't have children, but just because her sister didn't show any signs of being a mage doesn't mean she or her daughter didn't inherit it from the same ancestor."

Huh. Was there something to Aunt Clara's bones after all?

"However, I did consider you as well. Briefly."

"Flattering," I deadpanned.

"Yes. But you have a greater purpose in our endgame."

"A sacrifice?" I asked as scathingly as I could.

"Yes."

It wasn't Ida who answered me. It was a male voice, sonorous and deep, carrying from the door. Fear crept to my bones as I realised who it had to be.

Blackhart.

He walked to the foot of the altar, standing so I could get a good look even though I couldn't lift my head properly.

I studied him, trying to hide my fear. He wasn't at all what I'd imagined based on what I'd heard of him, and his voice. He could build a cult following on that voice.

It would probably end in a mass suicide or some other tragedy, but the people would go willingly just to hear him speak.

He was younger than I'd thought, not much past forty if that. He wore a black turtleneck with a black blazer, which was highly unimaginative. The altar blocked the rest, but the torso was slim and somewhat gaunt. Average height, certainly not much taller than Ida who stood next to him; narrow features, strawberry blond hair cut short to trim the curls, and such pale eyebrows they almost disappeared. It was a pleasant face, not handsome or remarkable, but one I might favour on a dating app if I was in a good mood.

And then his thin lips curled into a sneer. His pale blue eyes studied me with such coldness I was sure frost covered me. He wasn't merely an average man anymore. He was a person to be reckoned with, a power to be feared.

Saved by the Spell

Evil power.

"Good evening, Miss Thorpe. Glad you could join us."

"The pleasure is all yours."

He laughed, the sound cold despite his mellifluous voice, which was easily his best feature. I guess all evil mages weren't charming.

And I couldn't believe I was comparing a warlock favourably to him.

"I believe my sister has explained to you what is going to happen?"

His accent was cultured, which wasn't a surprise if the manor belonged to him. He had likely received the best of British private education available for the male gender.

I imagined him speaking in a heavy northern dialect—Geordie, because that was the only northern accent I knew—and a snicker escaped my mouth. I put it down to nerves.

His pale brows shot up. "You find your death funny?"

I bit the inside of my cheek, the spot that was already bleeding, and the pain grounded me. "I find the idea of you as a warlock funny. I've met one and you badly pale in comparison."

"Not after I've ascended."

"Descended, you mean. Keep fooling yourself. You'll never be the power you wish to be."

He leaned closer over my legs. "Unfortunately, you won't be here to see how wrong you are."

I forced a smile on my face. "There is a silver lining in everything."

Abruptly, he pulled away from the altar. I thought my remark had won the day for me, but it was merely my repulsiveness that had achieved the trick.

"What is this?" he asked Ida, making a sweeping gesture that encompassed my prone form. The disgusted flare of his nostrils was familiar to me, as I'd seen it on the faces of every man these past ten days.

"It's a medieval spell that makes her repulsive to men," Ida explained hastily.

"Why?"

I found it interesting that she hadn't told him about it.

Before she could answer, I pitched in: "She wanted to make your life more difficult for favouring Danielle over her."

I felt smug all of five seconds. Then she slapped me again. "That is not true." She shot a pleading look at him. "It's not. It was meant to weaken Mage Kane."

"Well, now it's weakening me," he drawled. "Take it off."

There was regret on her face she hadn't shown for me. "There's no counter-spell."

"There must be," I pleaded, although I should have kept my mouth shut. "How would fathers break the spell on their daughters when they married?"

Ida spared me a glance, her attention returning to Blackhart even before she answered, as if he were the magnet to her existence. The devotion on her face would have been creepy if she'd been his biological sister. Now it was merely … sad.

"Women with the spell on them never married. They were sent to convents."

That did not sound promising for me. I could never survive in a convent. Were there even any in Britain? I'd have to move to France, or Italy…

I wasn't even Catholic!

Saved by the Spell

I gave myself a mental slap and was able to focus again.

Blackhart furrowed his brows, not at all happy with her answer. "I can't perform the ritual if there's even a slightest distraction. And this is more than slight."

My breathing caught as hope returned. Would I be saved by the spell that had made my life a living hell?

And then I had to go and ruin it. "Rupert believed a true love's kiss would break it."

They pivoted to me like I'd yanked them.

Ida tilted her head, considering me. "Pity you're only attracted to cheating bastards. Otherwise, we could've tried it."

Ouch.

"You're the one who pushed me to Jack."

She smirked. "Please, as if you needed pushing."

That was embarrassingly true, though in my defence I'd spent the week before repulsing every man I even glanced at.

"Take her down," Blackhart ordered. "We'll use the other one."

What other one?

But before I could ask it aloud, Ida levitated me to the floor, dropping me from higher than was strictly necessary. If I survived this, my entire backside would be one big bruise.

My brain might never recover from the hits to my head.

Again, the levitation spell had drained her and her hold of the spell that kept me immobile loosened. I was able to squeeze my hands into fists, and wiggle my feet. Maybe even more, but I was afraid to try, in case they noticed.

Ida left the room with a clicking of her heels. Blackhart went with her, and I began to test the limits of my movements. I couldn't sit up yet, let alone walk, but I was able to move my arms properly.

If one of them came within punching distance, I'd be ready.

The spell's hold kept weakening, as if she was using her energy for other spells. In mere moments I was able to sit.

Before I had a chance to try standing, I heard Ida's clicking steps approach, and I lay hastily down again, making sure my braid wasn't under me this time.

She and Blackhart returned, and they weren't alone. They were dragging immobile figures by invisible leashes, Ida one and Blackhart two.

I strained my eyes to recognise them—and my heart stopped.

My friends.

Twenty-one

Ida and Blackhart brought my friends to the side of the room and levitated them to a standing position before lowering them onto their feet. Their eyes focused on me, growing large in shock when they realised who I was—and where I was. I gave them a thumbs-up behind Ida's and Blackhart's backs.

It didn't lessen their worry.

Only Kane, Giselle, and Amber were there, and my gut tightened. Where was Luca? And Rupert? I hoped they weren't hurt—or worse. Maybe the portal had taken them to a different place.

Maybe they were even now trying to find a way to us.

"What's the meaning of this?" Kane demanded. He looked physically fine, except for the part where he couldn't move his body. His voice filled me with confidence that we'd survive this. We might all be captive, but we'd find a way.

"Council Leader Kane," Blackhart said with a small bow. "I'm Julius Blackhart, and I will be the next archmage of London."

"What have you done to Rupert?" Amber demanded, and had her mouth sealed for her trouble, the flicker of Blackhart's fingers barely noticeable.

"Rupert needs to ponder on his choices a little longer," he answered with a smirk.

"He'll never concede the powers of the archmage to you," Kane stated.

I found the remark interesting. One apparently couldn't just kill the previous archmage and take their place. The power needed to be transferred, likely with some sort of spell. A good precaution, to be sure.

"Once I've ascended, there's no need for him to concede," Blackhart countered. He sounded confident, but I had a sudden notion that he wasn't correct. If any warlock could just take over an archmage's powers, they'd all be warlocks by now.

Giselle glowered at him. "What do you want with us?"

"My good madam, I don't want anything with you, but since you're here, you're going to help me." He gestured at me. "It appears my associates in their haste used a spell on Miss Thorpe that renders her unsuitable for my purposes."

"She makes you want to throw up," Giselle said, looking viciously pleased. She glanced at me. "I told you the spell would be more useful than you thought."

I smiled at her, though it was somewhat wobbly for sudden tears.

Blackhart sneered. "Unfortunately for you, Mrs Lynn, you're not protected by the spell. So you'll have to serve as the sacrifice for my ascension in her stead."

Giselle blanched, and she probably would have staggered back if she could have moved.

"No!"

Saved by the Spell

The magical power in Kane's voice made the chandeliers rattle. Ida winced, but Blackhart was unaffected.

"No?"

"You will not touch any of these women."

"And how do you propose you stop me? Even if I allowed you to use that voice again, which I won't, I have your vampire friend held as insurance."

Like Dufort earlier, Blackhart stretched his hand before him, open palm facing forward as if he were stopping incoming traffic, and made a circle in the air with it.

A portal opened. Since his back was turned to me, I risked lifting my head to see what was on the other side.

It opened to outside Catacomb Terraces, in front of the Sanford crypt. Lying on the lawn, spreadeagled and naked, was Luca. He looked unconscious and immobile.

"Luca!" I screamed, but if my voice carried to the other side of the portal, he didn't hear it, and he didn't stir.

The portal closed.

"The catacombs are wonderfully situated," Blackhart said, as if he were a tour guide. "The prospect is to east and the rising sun. At the top of the hill like it is, the sun will hit your friend long before the cemetery opens tomorrow morning. By then, there'll be only ashes left of him."

Bile rose to my mouth for fear for him. Even if we somehow managed to defeat Blackhart before sunrise, there was no way we could reach London without the portals, which we didn't know how to use.

"Either you do exactly as I say or your friend dies an agonising death." He regarded us with contempt. "Were it my choice, I'd let the vile creature die. But I understand you're fond of him."

"Yes," I said, my voice shaking a little.

"What will it be, then, Mrs Lynn? Will you sacrifice yourself for your friend?"

It was a horrible choice to ask of anyone, but Giselle didn't hesitate. "Yes."

Amber struggled against the invisible binding around her mouth, tears spilling from her eyes. Giselle tried to look at her, but she couldn't turn her head.

"I'm sorry, my love," she said to her wife. "But I couldn't live with myself if I let him die in my stead."

Part of me understood her. Part of me was frantically reaching for a solution where she didn't have to die either.

And then Kane made the choice for us.

"I'll be your sacrifice."

"No!" Giselle and I yelled. Amber frowned with fury, struggling to add her voice to ours too.

Blackhart sneered. "Thank you, Mage Kane. I must say, I'd much prefer you as a sacrifice. Unfortunately, I need you yet. Though not with a voice." He flickered his fingers, and even though I could see Kane's mouth moving, nothing came out. "Mrs Lynn, if you will."

He made a yanking gesture with his hand and Giselle flew across the floor, coming to an abrupt stop right in front of him. Her eyes were large with fright, and sweat glistened on her forehead.

"Yes ... you'll do." He glanced at Ida. "Prepare her."

With that, he walked out of the room, not glancing back.

If it annoyed Ida to be left with the mundane task again, she didn't show it. She made a motion with her hand and Giselle fell on her back, halting inches from the floor, before levitating onto the altar above me.

Ida's hold of my binding spell broke.

~ ~ ~

MY BODY WAS SUDDENLY subject to gravity again. I felt heavier, and I only barely managed to keep a gasp in as air escaped from my lungs.

I lay stock still, not wanting to draw Ida's attention, contemplating my options. Could I take Ida if I surprised her?

I had no fighting skills to speak of and no magic. I couldn't rely on the others to break their spells either, because they were most likely controlled by Blackhart, and good luck with his strength weakening.

Even if I could defeat her, there was Blackhart to reckon with. He wasn't large and strong looking, but I knew he had tricks in his arsenal that he could use for defeating me without even breaking a sweat.

I had to bide my time, then, and use it wisely.

Above me, Ida began to prepare Giselle for the ritual. Her attention was on her task, but I couldn't risk it.

"Do you need me down here?" I asked her, and she paused, as if she'd forgotten I existed. With a sweep of her arm, she sent me gliding across the floor with such force that I didn't stop until I hit the wall.

At least this time I was able to bend my body so that I didn't hit my head again.

I lay on the floor, on my side for a change. I kept pretending I was still bound by her spell, and she ignored me again. Once I was sure her attention was on her task, I inched closer to Kane and Amber, so that I would be shielded by their prone bodies.

"I have a plan," I said in a low voice. If they heard it, they didn't react. Of course, neither of them could speak. "I'm calling in the cavalry."

Or whatever the werewolf equivalent of it was. Lupinery.

With the clicking of her heels, Ida headed to the other end of the large room, which I could finally see properly, thanks to my new position. Workbenches and shelves full of books and other items necessary for spells filled the narrow end, and she began to collect what she needed.

Keeping one ear on the handy sound of her heels as she walked up and down the shelves, I dug out my phone from my back pocket. Amazingly, it hadn't suffered from the constant drops, it still had juice left, and there was good reception.

As fast as possible, I composed a message to Ashley:
```
Head to Highgate Cemetery. Terrace
Catacombs. Save Luca bf sunrise.
```
Ida returned to the altar before I could hit send, and I had to lay still. She began to purify Giselle—or something involving burning herbs—and the moment her back was turned to me, I sent the message.

Then I remembered the state she'd been in when we left home. She could recover fast, but maybe she was sleeping and wouldn't see the message until morning.

The mere thought turned my body cold.

I hit the call button and let it ring and ring, and when it stopped, I hit the button again. On the third round it connected, and I ended the call hastily, before her voice sounded in the room. I could only hope she read the message before calling back, but just in case, I kept my finger ready if the mobile began to ring.

Saved by the Spell

And ring it did, though only on vibrate. Since I was holding the phone, the sound was barely audible, and Ida didn't have supernatural hearing, but I disconnected hastily. A moment later a message arrived.

```
Da fuck?
```

Short and to the point as always. I had to wait until Ida headed to the other end of the room again, this time to fetch huge black candles, before sending an answer:

```
We're in deep trouble. Do not
call. Save Luca.
```

I hoped it was enough, because I had to switch the phone off. I couldn't risk it ringing again.

After that, there was nothing I could do but watch Ida prepare the ritual. I flexed my muscles every time her back was turned, willing them to be ready for action.

The altar was tall, and solid marble, like I'd suspected; long enough for a person my height and wide enough for Giselle to fit on it properly. Giselle remained silent while Ida drew a series of geometrical symbols around the altar with black chalk, but her breathing was ragged.

Once the symbols were done, Ida placed the candles on several spots over the altar. Then, with frightening efficiency like a trauma nurse—and wasn't that ironic—she cut Giselle's shirt open at the front, including the bra, baring her chest. She fetched two jars of salves and began to anoint her chest with them. They had such a pungent smell it made my nose itch all the way over on the side of the room.

Giselle began to cry softly. I wanted to console her, tell her we would rescue her, but I couldn't risk Ida noticing that I was free.

I had no idea how we would free her, but we would.

Finally, everything was ready. Ida left the room, trusting her spells to keep us in place. The moment the door closed behind her, I shot up. My legs held, which was pretty much the only thing going for me.

I rushed to the other end of the room and began to search for weapons I could hide on my body. I briefed my friends as I did.

"I've contacted Ashley. She'll save Luca." I had absolutely no doubt about it. Even if she couldn't move yet, she'd send someone else. "That leaves Rupert."

I stashed a flick-knife into my pocket, and slipped a longer knife up my sleeve where it sat snugly. I hoped it was the one Blackhart needed in his ritual.

"And us," Giselle noted in a teary voice. "Let's face it, with Kane's voice and body bound, there's nothing we can do against Blackhart."

"I can bloody well try."

"You can't attack them," she pointed out.

"No, but I can stall the ritual."

Just then, Kane growled. "I can speak again."

Relief washed through me, making my knees weak as I returned to my spot next to him and Amber.

"Thank God. Can you unbind yourself?"

"I can bloody well try," he echoed my words.

"But don't let them see," I hastily added, when I heard sounds outside the door. I settled back down, making sure my braid wasn't stuck under me.

"Why the hell not?" he demanded.

"We need the element of surprise. Keep quiet."

I'd never ordered my boss around like this, but then again, we'd never been in a situation quite like this either.

The double doors at the other end of the room flew open, probably moved by magic. The chandeliers that had illuminated the room with blinding force died, plunging the room into darkness. The candles around the altar

Saved by the Spell

flared to life, as did several other candles around the room.

Dramatic much?

Despite my sarcastic attitude, my palms turned sweaty with fear when Blackhart and Ida entered. They'd changed into black, floor-length robes, and covered their faces with black half-masks, as if we didn't know who they were. Both were barefooted.

They progressed to the altar at a dignified pace, and I half expected Bach's *Toccata and Fugue in D minor* to blast from a hidden organ somewhere.

Blackhart took position on the far side of the altar, facing us, and Ida paused at its foot. They stood silent for a moment, concentrating. Then she presented him with a silver dagger—so mine wasn't it after all—offering it with both hands.

He accepted it silently, turned to Giselle, who was crying again, and lifted the dagger above his head as if preparing to strike.

"No!"

The shout was out of my mouth before I had a chance to consider the wisdom of it. But I hadn't thought he'd just kill her. Weren't there any preparations? Spells or incantations first?

An invisible punch in my stomach left me gasping for air. "Do not interrupt me. The slightest distraction will assure that the ritual won't work and then your friend will have died for nothing."

I gritted my teeth, forcing the words out. "Her cooperation rests on knowing that Luca is freed."

"I lied."

Bastard. I should have seen that coming.

"But you still need Kane's cooperation. If you kill Giselle, he'll never concede the council to Ida." I paused when a realisation hit. "That was never your intention, was it? You want to rule London without her."

"What?" Ida looked stunned, then angry. "You would exclude me?"

"Of course I won't," he said impatiently, and I snorted.

"Of course he will. Why else would he make sure that you'll have no chance taking over London?"

"He'll die and she'll rule," Blackhart stated.

I pushed on my knees, no longer caring if they knew I could move. "That's not how it goes and you know it. The magic that protects London has to recognise the leader. And it'll rule for the winner of the challenge."

I stood up, straightening my spine. "And as you can see, she's not even strong enough to control me. How do you think she'll best him?"

From the corner of my eye, I saw Kane squeeze his hand into a fist, preparing an energy ball. Knowing that he could move again bolstered my confidence, but I couldn't let him attack her just yet. I needed a portal to London.

"I'll defeat him now," Ida stated with confidence, stepping closer. Her hand formed a fist too, signalling an immediate attack.

"That won't help you," I halted her hastily. "The magic isn't here. It's in London. You'll have to defeat him there."

She glowered at me. "If you think I'll travel all the way to London now, you're delusional."

Saved by the Spell

I sneered back, amazed she hadn't tried to bind me with the spell again, but I guess she needed to conserve her strength.

"And here I thought you can conjure portals."

"Enough," Blackhart shouted, and I felt my mouth being sealed with magic.

Bugger. But at least my body still moved.

He took a tighter hold of the dagger again, preparing for the strike. I tensed, trying to judge if I could rush at him in time to stop it, but before I could move, Ida spoke:

"I want you to open the portal to London before we proceed."

Twenty-two

"EXCUSE ME?" THE LOOK ON Blackhart's face didn't promise anything good for Ida, but she stood her ground.

"Phoebe's right. Kane won't concede the council to me, and I can't fight him here. I need to be sure you value my contribution to the cause enough to grant me this favour."

He stared at her with contempt. "And why would I want you to rule the council? I won't even need the council once I'm the archmage."

"You need the council spell to recognise you. It won't do it once you're the archmage, because that's how it's supposed to work. You need me to rule the council."

"I could use Jack."

Ida's face distorted with anger. "He already challenged Kane and lost. He won't be able to try again for another two years."

The flames of the candles surged up with his flaring rage, but he gained control immediately.

"Fine."

With a circle of his open palm, he opened the portal, choosing the cemetery again. The scene was still the same, Luca lying unconscious on the grass. Ashley hadn't reached him yet, but it hadn't been all that long since I alerted her.

A yank of his hand sent Kane flying through the portal. He landed on his feet not far from Luca, facing the portal. He didn't move, and I feared Blackhart had tightened the binding spell on him again. He would never be able to release himself in time before Ida attacked.

"I'll keep your friends on this side to make sure of your cooperation," he said to Kane. I felt myself being yanked through the air to stand behind him. Amber landed on his other side.

I was on my feet again, and fortunately for me, Blackhart hadn't thought to renew the binds. I considered surging through the portal, but that would only hurt my friends.

He turned to bow at his sister. The sneer on his face was mocking. "Your opponent awaits. Make me proud."

Ida pulled herself straight and with as much dignity as it was possible when wearing a robe and bare feet, she walked through the portal.

The moment their backs were turned on me, I glanced around for a weapon. I had the dagger, but now that I was close enough to Blackhart to use it, I knew with absolute certainty that I couldn't. I would have to aim to kill, because if I didn't, he would defeat me with magic. And I wasn't a killer, not even in self-defence.

My eyes alighted on the large black candle next to me. It was easily three feet tall solid wax that stood without support of a candleholder, and hefty enough to need both hands to wrap around it.

Saved by the Spell

I'd have to act fast, while his attention was on the scene on the other side of the portal. I picked up the candle, marvelling at its weight, just as Ida threw a blue energy ball at Kane.

I froze in fear as it shot through the air at him. But at the last possible moment, Kane stepped aside and threw an energy ball of his own, with much greater force and accuracy.

It hit Ida straight in the chest and she fell on her back, unconscious.

Blackhart roared. He conjured a huge energy ball and threw it through the portal with all the force of his rage.

Brandishing the candle, I hit him at the back of his head with the full force of mine. I used the sharp-edged bottom, like a battering ram, ignoring the hot molten wax dripping on me. The soft material of the candle cushioned the blow, but my aim was true and strong.

He collapsed to the floor, unconscious.

The portal died. The last thing I saw before it did was Blackhart's energy ball hit Kane squarely in the chest.

I hit his head again.

~ ~ ~

WITH BLACKHART UNCONSCIOUS, the spell binding Amber disappeared so abruptly that she fell to her knees. She recovered fast and pushed up.

I stood above Blackhart, the huge candle ready, in case I needed to hit him again, but he stayed down. Amber made a move with her hands and then leaned over to try his pulse.

"He's alive and I've bound him with magic."

"We'll bind him with actual ropes too, because he's too skilled to be held down with magic for long."

I headed to the shelves at the other end to look for ropes, and Amber rushed to help Giselle down from the altar. When I glanced back, they were hugging and kissing tightly.

There were no ropes on the shelves, but the long velvet curtains were held back by golden ropes with long tassels. As fast as I could, I began to remove them, hoping they'd be long enough to keep Blackhart down. I didn't ask for help, even though it would have been faster. Giselle and Amber needed their moment.

By the time I carried the bundle of ropes to Blackhart, Giselle had put on Amber's T-shirt, as Amber still had her coat. It was tight on her, but better than walking around bare-breasted, with odd symbols drawn on her skin.

Together, we tied Blackhart's hands behind his back, his legs together, and for a further measure, tied his arms to his legs, pulling his body backwards like a bow.

Turned out, his robe was open at the front and he wasn't wearing anything underneath—gag—so we took one more rope and used it to secure the hem of the rope to his thighs.

"There," Amber said with vicious satisfaction. "Now we need to find a place that'll hold him."

I nodded, picturing the most horrifying place I could think of. "Pity we can't get him to the sarcophagus where he held Rupert."

"Rupert!" Giselle exclaimed, throwing her hands on her cheeks in horror. "We have to find him."

Amber nodded. "Let's take this one with us, and swap their places."

She made the flicker with her wrist I already associated with the levitation spell, and Blackhart rose from the

Saved by the Spell

floor. She headed out of the ballroom, and he hovered behind him, face down and body bent.

"Where should we look for him?" I asked.

"We were kept in the cellar, so I think we'll start there," Giselle said, heading down the stairs.

Amber wasn't as careful as Ida had been levitating Blackhart, and he slid down the stairs at breakneck speed, stopping face first on the landing with a satisfying thud.

"Oops," Amber snickered, but she slowed his descent down the next flight.

We were in a grand entrance hall. In any other situation I would have stopped to gawp and admire the elegant space and the wonderful original furniture from the eighteenth century. But I hurried after Amber and Giselle, and the still unconscious Blackhart, to the back of the house and the kitchen there.

It was dark at that time of night, but Giselle located the light switch and flicked them on. The interior was like straight from a century ago, only everything was modern, the entire space refurbished with retro appliances and furniture.

"Nice," Giselle said, and I agreed. Not that I ever cooked.

The door to the cellar was next to the pantry, and original by the look of it. It opened soundlessly though, and the electric fixtures on the other side were less than two decades old.

We headed down the concrete steps, with Amber slowing Blackhart's descent by holding the ropes binding him. The cellar was typical of houses of this age, which were mostly used for storing food and coal. This one, though, held wine racks on one wall and dried herbs and such on the other. The back wall had a washer and a dryer, which I thought was rather mundane, but I guess warlocks in making needed their clothes washed like everyone else.

I distracted myself briefly by wondering if he did his washing himself or if he employed a housekeeper.

Amber let go of the hovering spell and Blackhart dropped to the floor. "We were held here. I think Rupert is behind that door."

The last wall held a blast door, the kind that were on boiler rooms in case of fire. It didn't have a lock on it, but I didn't doubt for a moment that it would be impossible to open.

"Does it have similar wards as the crypt door?"

A snicker sounded from the floor, turning into mad laughter. "Good luck getting through those."

We pivoted to Blackhart, who was staring at us with murder in his eyes.

"How are you awake?" I demanded angrily. At least the ropes still held.

"I was awake before we left the ballroom. You'll pay for the insult of dropping me."

"I'm shivering in fear," Amber said.

"You should. It's a matter of moment before I'm free."

"Not if you can't speak," she countered, and sealed his mouth with a sweeping motion of her hand.

"I didn't know you were such a powerful mage," I said admiringly.

She shrugged, but looked pleased. "I'm not as good as Archibald, but I have my skills." She turned to face the door. "Now, let's see what you're made of."

Saved by the Spell

She didn't need to look long. "These are the same as on the crypt. Only, with the black magic wards still in place."

My shoulders slumped and Giselle got tears in her eyes. "How will we get Rupert free?"

"Maybe he's not even there," I suggested hesitantly. "We'd be wasting our time."

"Rupert! If you can hear us, bang on the door," Amber bellowed.

Nothing happened.

"Maybe there are wards on that side too, and he can't touch the door," Giselle said, worry evident in her kind eyes.

Then a metallic clang sounded from the inside and we jumped, partly in sudden startle, partly in relief.

"Hang on, Rupert," Amber shouted. "We're trying to figure out how to take down the wards."

I bit my lip. "Should I try to call Dufort again? He broke the wards the last time."

"No!" the women said in unison.

"He can't be relied on any more than that bastard can," Amber said, pointing at Blackhart.

"Besides, it's long past midnight even in France," Giselle pointed out. "He wouldn't be happy if you woke him up for a favour."

That I could readily believe. The point was moot anyway, as I didn't have Danielle's number.

"We have to do something." I crossed my arms over my chest in frustration—and felt the dagger I'd hidden inside my sleeve.

I'd completely forgotten it. It wasn't large and my sleeve was tight, so it sat snugly inside it, almost unnoticeable once the metal had grown warm against my skin.

I pulled it out, brandishing it. Giselle and Amber pulled back. Amber glared at me.

"What do you think that'll achieve?"

"You can't force him to unravel the wards," Giselle added. "He needs his hands for it, and that would be paramount to freeing him."

"I know that. But I have to try something."

I studied the trussed-up man on the floor. He was immobile, or pretending to be, but his eyes were fixed on the dagger. Was it a magical dagger? One that would force him to do our bidding? Whatever it was, his face was gaunt with worry.

And then I remembered: "Blood!" That's what Dufort had told me, but I'd been too tense to properly listen. "The wards can be taken down by using the blood of the caster."

Blackhart's eyes flashed in impotent fury, and I knew I was right.

"That's disgusting," Giselle said, but Amber was a former trauma nurse, and she didn't flinch.

"That's black magic for you. He truly is a step away from becoming a warlock. I'll get a cup."

She rushed up the steps to the kitchen and soon returned with a shallow bowl that looked like it was made for bleeding a person.

She also carried a first-aid kit. I guess we weren't going to let Blackhart bleed to death.

She kneeled by him and held out a hand for me. "I'll do it. You might cut something vital."

Since she was right, and I didn't want to do it anyway, I gladly gave up the dagger.

Saved by the Spell

She cut the rope keeping Blackhart's arms bound to his legs, and his legs fell straight with a thump. He couldn't speak, but I could see the relief on his face and didn't like it.

She turned him on his side, left side up. Then she pulled up his left sleeve, chose a spot on the crook of his arm, and sprayed it with antiseptic spray she'd taken from the first-aid kit. Then, like the nurse she was, she used a magical flame to disinfect the dagger as well, before making a precise but deep cut into the vein there.

Blood welled instantly, and she put the bowl under it.

"How much do you think we'll need?" she asked after a while. "There's only so much we can remove before it'll damage him."

"I'm not feeling charitable, so take all you can," I stated. Blackhart glowered furiously in return, but the binding on his mouth and body held.

Amber kept a finger on his pulse. When she deemed it was slowing down too much, she sealed the cut with magic, and handed me the bowl of blood, before proceeding to clean and bind the wound with more mundane means. It was soon done, and she stood up, walking to her wife, placing a hand on her shoulder.

I held the bowl gingerly. I didn't want to get any of it on me. "How do you think it's done?"

Giselle had been studying the wards the whole time, and she turned to take the bowl from me. "Step back."

Amber and I obeyed hastily. Giselle took a hold of the edge of the bowl, and before I knew what she was up to, she threw the blood against the door.

A loud explosion assaulted my ears, making them ring. Smoke began to waft from the wards on the wall, made visible by the blood, and a horrible stench of burning blood filled the room.

The smoke made tears fall from my eyes, and I gagged, but nothing seemed to rid the smell.

The smoke faded mercifully fast once the blood had burned the wards away. The stench lingered though.

Giselle studied the door with a tilted head. Then she nodded, and reached for the door handle. Nothing happened, and she pulled the door open.

Rupert stood on the other side. "Well done. Now, where's that bastard?"

We stepped aside to show him Blackhart's trussed up form.

He wasn't there.

Only the ropes remained where Blackhart had been, burned through. "What the hell?"

I walked closer, staring at the spot where he had lain, as if he would miraculously materialise. I kicked it for the further measure, just in case he had made himself invisible, but my leg only met air, almost making me fall.

"You let him flee?" Rupert demanded angrily, but Amber was having none of that.

"We didn't let him do anything. He's a powerful mage who had more tricks up his sleeve than we believed possible. He must've created a portal."

"He could be anywhere," Giselle said, upset, but I had a more horrifying thought.

"He could be at Highgate Cemetery!"

The women inhaled sharply, but Rupert shot me an annoyed look. "Why would he go there when we know that's where his hideout is?"

Saved by the Spell

"Kane is there, and he's injured. And Ida too, his accomplice. He wants Ida to defeat Kane to take over the London council."

His eyes bulged in outrage. "Well, don't just stand there. Let's go help him. You call a cab."

Amber and Giselle headed up the stairs with Rupert, but I halted them. "I don't think you understand. We're not in London."

They turned to stare at me, amazed. "Where in the blazes are we, then?" Rupert demanded impatiently.

"York."

Giselle let out a wail. "We'll never get to London in time."

"We will if we use a portal too."

Amber put her arms on her hips, giving me a stern look. "I already told you we are not calling Dufort."

I shook my head. "There's the permanent portal here that leads to the cemetery. And Rupert knows how to open it."

They looked instantly more hopeful. "We weren't conscious when we were brought from there to here," Amber said. "This place is huge. We might spend hours searching for it."

"I know where it is," I stated. "Follow me."

Twenty-three

I HEADED UP THE STAIRS WITH MORE energy than I should have left after the night we'd had. We crossed the kitchen and hurried down the hallway to the staircase. There probably were stairs from the kitchen too, but I thought it best to trace the route Ida had taken me.

Two flights of stairs up and everyone was winded, although Rupert was doing extremely well for his age and after his ordeals. I had no idea what sort of magic he used for it, but I wanted some.

The hallway to the other end of the house seemed shorter now that I was walking, and we soon reached the room where the portal was.

Rupert walked in first. "Let me see."

He concentrated, and like before, gathered enough magic to trigger the portal to open. It was as impressive as the first time, but he did look more tired afterwards as we hurried through. We needed to get him home as fast as possible.

But first, we needed to get into the tunnel and out of the sarcophagus. With the mages' light balls illuminating the way, the place didn't seem at all frightening.

"Did Ida find you here?" Amber asked as we crossed the cellar, the portal closing behind us.

"No, I managed to get back to the crypt and she was waiting for me there. She's the one who had the tracking spell on me."

I'd have to ask them to remove it as soon as possible.

At the top of the steps, I had to search for the right brick again, but it was faster this time. I pressed it down and the sarcophagus glided aside. My sigh of relief revealed how worried I'd been that it wouldn't.

Amber halted us. "I'll go first, in case Ida is waiting for us again."

"Shouldn't I go first in that case?" Rupert enquired, but she shook her head.

"We'll need you for Blackhart, if he's here."

She climbed out, and gave us an all clear immediately. "We need to hurry. I think there's a battle outside."

We clambered out of the stairs and hurried across the small crypt. Amber opened the door carefully and we peered out. I gasped in shock.

The night was dark, the moon already setting, but there were a couple of mage lights illuminating the scene.

Kane and Ida were battling, and by the looks of it, had been for some time. The front of his shirt was burned away, likely already by Blackhart's spell, and there was a nasty burn mark on his chest. He was clearly in pain, and moving much slower than usual. His energy balls were smaller too, and his throws weren't as accurate.

Ida wasn't doing well either, but she had the upper hand. Kane was falling back, and she was advancing with a volley of energy balls that he barely managed to dodge.

"Concede!" she screamed.

"Never!"

Saved by the Spell

Pride swelled in my chest.

"Your friends are dead. You have nothing to fight for."

"I have London and the mages here to fight for. And I know my friends aren't dead."

"You only hope so," she screeched, flinging an energy ball that hit him on the shoulder of his throwing arm. That wasn't good.

I rushed out of the door. "We're alive!"

My shout distracted them both, but Kane recovered faster.

Using the last of his energy, he conjured a large ball and bowled it at her as if the English cricket glory relied on him in a Test match. It hit her in stomach and she flew back with force, falling on her back. Before she could climb on her feet, Kane had her immobilised with the binding spell.

He staggered with exhaustion, and I rushed to him, managing to catch him before he fell. He was heavier than I anticipated, but I was able to hold him up.

"Thank you," he said, straightening and pulling away.

My heart ached. If Ida was right, I'd never get the spell lifted, and I'd repulse him for the rest of my life.

"This does not end here!" Ida screeched. She made to get up, but Kane's binding held—for now. Exhausted as he was, it was only a matter of time before she freed herself.

A large grey wolf surged out of the shadows and stood above her, growling. Ashley!

Only then did I realise that Luca wasn't there anymore. Ashley must have reached him in time, or his bindings had disappeared when Blackhart passed out and he'd managed to move to safety on his own.

253

Kane walked to Ida and stood above her, staring down.

"In front of these witnesses, you challenged me for the leadership of the council of mages, yes?" he began the now familiar formula.

"Go to hell."

He gave her a level look. "I've invoked the spell. It has to be followed through. Answer the question."

"Yes," she spat.

"In front of these witnesses, your challenge was accepted, yes?"

Her jaw tightened as she ground her teeth together. "Yes."

"And in front of these witnesses, I won and you lost, yes?"

This time I was certain she wouldn't answer, but Ashley growled, and she nodded. "Yes."

"As I free you, you agree not to challenge me again during this cycle?"

"I'll never agree to that!"

Kane cocked an inquiring brow. "Are you sure? It'll be a long eternity bound like that. And it won't be me holding you, it'll be the entire London. Good luck breaking that spell."

She growled, and Ashley growled in return. Hers was more impressive.

"I'll ask you again," Kane said. "Will you agree not to challenge me again during this cycle?"

"Yes." She shouted the word with all her anger. "But don't for a moment think you've won. Julius will defeat you."

Kane nodded. "So be it."

Saved by the Spell

He moved his fingers, releasing her. He held a hand to her to help her up, but she refused it and pushed to her feet.

"Am I free to leave?" she asked scathingly, and Kane stepped aside, making a sweeping gesture towards the path down. We turned with him—and froze in horror.

Jack was standing on the path below us. He was holding a gun, pointing it at Kane. "I think we'll negotiate the council leadership again."

Kane huffed, not at all frightened by the weapon. I could barely breathe; my heart was beating so hard.

"You cannot challenge me again."

Jack tilted his head. "No, but you can concede. I checked."

"For you?" Kane asked, his voice full of disbelief.

"Yes."

"What the fuck, Jack?" Ida demanded. "I'm the one who will lead."

"I'm not happy with that arrangement anymore."

"Neither of you will lead," Kane said, sounding surprisingly patient. "I won't concede to either of you. No matter what sort of gun you point at me."

"How about her, then?"

The gun turned to point at me.

~ ~ ~

KANE DIDN'T HESITATE. "Fine. Put the gun away."

I faced him, outraged. "Are you out of your mind?"

His look was very gentle and patient. "This isn't a great hardship for me. You're more important."

That did warm me, but I wasn't moved. "Think of the poor mages if Jack leads them."

"He'll lead no one," Ida shouted. "Julius chose me!"

I turned to her. "No, he didn't. He lied to you."

"He's just confused," she said, her jaw jutting up with stubbornness. "He'll recognise he needs my help."

I spread my arms. "Meanwhile, he fled, leaving you here, at the mercy of us—and the archmage."

Rupert was standing at the edge of the group, supported by Giselle. Age and exhaustion had finally caught up with him too. But now he straightened.

"Neither of you is fit to lead anyone, and Blackhart will soon be dealt with. I suggest you make yourselves scarce before I have to deal with you myself."

"No!" Jack roared. The gun was still pointed at me, but his hand was shaking. I feared he would fire it by accident. "Concede the council to me or I'll kill her."

Angry calm washed over me, and my skin tingled like when magic was gathering, my fury tightening it. I took a step closer to him and stared him down, defiantly. "Go ahead, kill me. Because of you, my life is ruined anyway. You might as well finish the job. But Kane will not concede to you or Ida."

Several things happened at once. A dark figure sprang from the foliage, superhumanly fast, and wrapped fingers around Jack's throat. I saw a flash of fangs, before my view was obstructed by Kane, who had thrown his body in front of me. He wrapped his arms around me, pressing me against his—bare!—chest. A shot rang out.

I stiffened with anticipated pain, but it didn't happen. Kane didn't collapse on me either, so the bullet hadn't hit either of us.

"I think you can let me go," I muttered against Kane's bare(!) chest. He glanced behind him, and released me. I tried not to be disappointed.

Saved by the Spell

"I don't think you should look," he said, so naturally I had to peer around him.

Part of me wished I hadn't. Luca had his arms wrapped around Jack's torso from behind, holding the unconscious man up effortlessly, while his fangs were sunk deep in his throat. His eyes were directed at us though, like a predator keeping an eye on challenges on his prey. They shone like emerald lights in the dark.

I glanced around for threats he might have perceived, but everything was secure. Ashley had Ida on the ground, fangs holding her throat lightly. If Ida tried anything funny, the wolf would bite through.

No one seemed injured, but Rupert was leaning on Amber exhausted. The shot must have gone wide.

Giselle walked gently closer to Luca, her hands in front of her in a calming gesture. "I think you've had enough, Luca," she said in an even tone. "Let him go."

At first it looked like he wouldn't comply. Then the fangs retreated, and he lifted his head, licking his lips.

"Mmm ... mage's blood." His voice was a low purr unlike I'd never heard from him before. It made the small hairs in my body stand. "That'll keep me for a year."

He licked the bite wounds on Jack's throat and they disappeared, as if they'd never been there. Then he lowered Jack to the ground, surprisingly gently, and stepped aside. Only then did I see that he was wearing what had to be Ashley's clothing, they were so large on him.

"What did I miss?"

Relieved laughter filled the night, as we all let go of the tension that had kept us in its grip for hours. We'd survived. Mostly unscathed too, if you didn't count the bruises on my body and Kane's burns.

I turned to him. He was smiling brightly, his deep blue eyes shining. Our gazes met, and he pulled me against him. I barely realised what was happening when he already lifted me closer and kissed me. Properly.

I was so stunned I didn't have a chance to react, and then it was over, and he pulled away.

I was flustered, but I refused to behave like a maiden, so I smiled. "I'm happy you're all right."

"It was a close shave." He smiled too. "If Ashley hadn't kept Ida in check until I gained consciousness, who knows what would've happened."

I glanced at where the wolf was still holding Ida down, reluctant to release her, despite Giselle's best efforts. My heart warmed and I felt tears prick my eyes.

Kane patted my shoulder, more formal again. "It's been a long night. Let's go home."

"Not so fast," Rupert stated. "There's the matter of your succession to consider."

Kane pulled straight, wincing when it made his burns hurt. "I'm not going anywhere, so I don't need a successor."

"Yes, you are. You'll become my apprentice like you should have done years ago. Blackhart is still out there, and I'll be damned if we're not ready to face him when he returns." He held his hands up when Kane looked like he would argue. "You're by far the best mage of your generation, and indeed the whole of London. You will not waste it on bureaucracy."

Giselle nodded. "Rupert is right. We need you as the future archmage more than we need you as the council leader."

"But who'll lead the council?" he asked, bewildered. "None of my challengers have succeeded so far."

Saved by the Spell

Rupert pointed at Amber, who stepped back in surprise. "She will. I'm amazed you haven't thought of it before now."

"The reason being that I haven't wanted to," Amber said dryly, but Rupert glared her from under his brows.

"Start wanting it, because that's how it'll be."

Giselle patted her wife's arm, looking proud. "You'll be brilliant."

I thought so too, but since this didn't require my input, I kept my mouth shut.

Amber wasn't backing down. "On one condition. You'll get a proper housekeeper and let Jones retire."

Rupert glared at her. "Fine. I want Giselle."

"Not going to happen. She's mine."

Giselle smiled. "I can come on Sundays to cook for you. For the rest, you'll hire someone permanent."

That pleased him and he nodded. "But no one annoying. I won't have anyone meddlesome in my home."

Shaking her head exasperatedly, Amber gave in. "Fine. If Archibald is willing?"

He ran fingers through his hair in indecision. "I hadn't thought to become an archmage, but Rupert is right. We need to prepare for Blackhart. If there's no one better…?" He gave Rupert a questioning look, and the old man shook his head.

"In that case, I agree." He turned to Amber with a challenging smile on his face and spread his arms. "But I'll be damned if I just concede."

Amber laughed, and with a flicker of her hand rendered him immobile. Then she pulled straight and there was power in her voice when she spoke:

"In front of these witnesses, I challenged you for the leadership of the council of mages, yes?"

"Yes," Kane answered with a steady voice.

"In front of these witnesses, my challenge was accepted, yes?"

"Yes."

"And in front of these witnesses, I won and you lost, yes?"

Kane smiled. "Yes."

"As I free you, you agree not to challenge me again during this cycle?"

"I agree."

"I am now the leader of the council of mages, yes?"

"Yes."

The world shook as the spell took hold. Power filled Amber, lifting her wildly curling hair, and making her pale blue eyes shine with an inner light. She stretched her fingers wide and tiny bolts of lightning shot between them.

"Wow," she said when everything settled down. "That was quite a rush."

Kane offered her his hand and they shook. "You'll make a great leader," he assured her. "Congratulations."

We all went to her, one by one hugging her. Her body buzzed against mine, as if it were charged with electricity.

"Well," she said when we'd settled down. "I guess we'd best head home, then."

"What should we do with Ida and Jack?" I asked, and she shook her head as if she'd forgotten about them.

"We're not in the business of incarcerating people, but they shouldn't go unpunished."

She went to Ida, who was still guarded by Ashley, but a signal from her made the wolf retreat and sit down next to her.

Saved by the Spell

"You are free to go, but you will not be able to perform magic in London anymore."

It was mild, as far as punishments went. Kane had threatened to rob mages of their magic for less. But that would render them useless for Blackhart's plans. Ida seemed to understand it, because her mouth tightened, but she nodded.

"So be it." She got up. "May I take Jack with me?"

Amber nodded, and Ida levitated Jack's prone form up. But instead of heading down the path, she went to the crypt. They would be out of London in no time.

My shoulders slumped in relief when the door closed behind them. "I hope that was the last we'll see of them."

Everyone nodded, but we wouldn't be holding our breath.

Amber and Giselle took Rupert home in Kane's car, and Kane went with them. Luca and I headed to Ashley's car farther down the street, having found the keys in the pocket of her clothes he was wearing. We were leaning heavily against each other for support. I was exhausted and he was drunk on Jack's blood, which made our journey slow and rather meandering. The wolf loped so close she brushed my legs from time to time, threatening to trip me.

I reached a hand and rubbed her ears. She let me, as evidenced by the fact that I got to keep my hand.

At the car, we let Ashley into the back, and I took the wheel. Luca climbed into the passenger seat.

"Shouldn't you sit in the back, so I won't repulse you?"

He gave it a thought. "No. I don't know if it's the mojo from the mage's blood or what, but you don't repulse me anymore. I think the spell's been broken."

As I started the car, I wondered if that could be true. And if it was, how it had come to be? I hoped it didn't mean Jack was dead. He'd made my life difficult, but I didn't wish him dead for it. But Blackhart needed his sacrifice, and he might do.

The other thought, that a kiss would have broken it, was too much to contemplate, so I didn't.

"Well, I'm glad to see it gone, even if it saved my life."

Luca grinned. "Saved by the repulsion spell. Who would've thought that?"

Who indeed?

Epilogue

OLIVIA CALLED ME THE NEXT DAY and told me the wedding was back on.

"It must've been some sort of brain episode like you said, because he remembered everything this morning and came back, so sweetly apologetic that I naturally forgave him. He had a cat-scan, and even though it didn't reveal anything alarming, we both agreed that we should get married as fast as possible."

I was happy for them, even though part of me wanted to reveal that they'd been manipulated into marrying. Their love had to be real anyway, as it couldn't be created by magic.

I wondered if the spell had broken because Jack had died, or because Ida had made him break it. I hoped the latter.

The wedding was held on Saturday the next week, and it was a much smaller affair than the pair had originally intended, because the groom's cousin and best man had gone mysteriously missing, and the pair didn't want to show disrespect with a large event.

My suggestion that Ida and Jack had eloped to Bahamas together and were happy in their romantic hideout didn't gather support—mostly because no one believed when I told they'd been an item. Henry's worry for them made the event subdued.

The ceremony was held mid-morning in a small church in Greenwich, where Olivia's parents lived, and only immediate family members attended, with me as the sole bridesmaid—in the blue dress, as my bruises had faded enough for it—and Henry's cousin from his mother's side standing for him. The bride was beautiful and radiant in Dior and the groom had eyes only for her. Everyone cried.

The wedding lunch was in a nearby restaurant we had for ourselves, and I made sure I was seated next to Aunt Clara. The moment I had a chance, I asked about Great-Aunt Beverly.

"Mom's sister?" she asked, puzzled. "What brought that about?"

"I went through old photos, and she was there," I gave the answer I'd thought of in advance. "What was she like?"

Her eyes clouded as she reminisced. "She was an independent woman at a time when it was discouraged. Of course, her generation of women often remained unmarried, as so many young men perished in the Second World War. And she had an amazing knowledge of herbs and traditional healing. She meant to teach me too, but then I married and had Emilia, and became too busy. It never came up later. But you know what? She was the only person who never made fun of my bones."

The happy couple headed for their honeymoon, a week in my parents' guesthouse in the south of France. It

Saved by the Spell

was a great destination for them, but it would mean Mother would redouble her efforts to get me to marry.

At least I had a chance for it now. Because Luca had been right. The spell was broken. The space I'd enjoyed in the Tube was gone, but I didn't care. I didn't have to spend the rest of my life in a convent.

And things were back to normal with Kane again. That is to say, slightly formal. But at least he didn't have the pained expression on his face anymore.

I wanted to bring the spell up, but we were insanely busy with the auction preparations. All his free time he spent either briefing Amber about running the council or heading to Rupert's to start learning with him.

It left me wondering if I'd imagined the kiss.

He greeted me with a warm smile when I entered the gallery for the auction. Thanks to the change in Olivia's wedding plans, I had time for both.

"You look lovely. I trust the wedding went well?"

I hadn't had time to go change, and I was wearing my wedding finery. And I still wouldn't be best-dressed person there, if past auctions were anything to judge by. Kane looked great in his black tie too.

The auctioneer arrived and we didn't have a chance to speak again until the auction was over. It was a great success, and we were in a wonderful mood as we followed Kane to a fine restaurant with Mrs Walsh, as was our tradition.

It wasn't until we were waiting for dessert and Mrs Walsh went to powder her nose that we were finally alone. Kane leaned back in his chair, his head tilted as he studied me.

"I'm sorry we haven't had a chance to go over what happened with Blackhart. I know it was traumatic, but you were brilliant, and I haven't even thanked you."

A light blush rose to my cheeks. "I didn't expect to be thanked."

He cleared his throat. "About that kiss…"

Here it was. My stomach tightened, but I smiled. "It was pleasant, but nothing you need to worry about. We weren't there as a boss and employee, so you didn't breach any rules."

He didn't look as relieved as I'd expected. He nodded. "That's good. But I more wanted to talk about how it was possible."

"I thought it was the relief brought it about…"

"But it wasn't the kiss that broke the spell."

It wasn't? My disappointment probably showed on my face, because he smiled.

"I wouldn't have been able to kiss you if the spell hadn't been broken already. I was in poor shape, having spent all my energy fighting Ida. At the best of times it took a great deal of it to be around you. I would've passed out if I'd tried to kiss you with the spell on."

He leaned his elbows on the table. "I've studied the spell carefully with Rupert, and we've come to the conclusion that it works differently on those who have magic in their blood."

I shook my head, uncomprehending. "I don't understand…"

My heart was thumping in my chest.

"There seems to be a failsafe in the spell. Those with magic in their blood should be able to break its hold on them by facing the caster. And you faced Jack. Spectacularly."

Saved by the Spell

He looked at me with admiration, but I still had no idea what he meant. His smile deepened.

"You, Phoebe Thorpe, are a mage."

Acknowledgements

Thank you, my readers, for receiving the first book in the House of Magic series so warmly, encouraging me to continue with Phoebe and her friends. This is for you.

And as always, I want to thank my family for their support and help. I couldn't do this without you.

About the Author

SUSANNA SHORE is an independent author of more than twenty books. She writes *Two-Natured London* paranormal romance series about vampires and wolf-shifters that roam London, and *P.I. Tracy Hayes* series of a Brooklyn waitress turned private investigator. She also writes stand-alone thrillers, and contemporary romances with billionaires and the strong women who love them. When she's not writing, she's reading or—should her husband manage to drag her outdoors—taking long walks.

www.susannashore.com

Made in United States
North Haven, CT
03 April 2023